MW01127528

# *The Warrior Code*

# The Warrior Code

## SEAL Strike Book Two

Martin L. Strong

iUniverse, Inc.
New York Lincoln Shanghai

The Warrior Code
SEAL Strike Book Two

All Rights Reserved © 2003 by Martin L. Strong


No part of this book may be reproduced or transmitted in any form or by
any means, graphic, electronic, or mechanical, including photocopying,
recording, taping, or by any information storage retrieval system, without the
written permission of the publisher.

iUniverse, Inc.


For information address:
iUniverse
2021 Pine Lake Road, Suite 100
Lincoln, NE 68512
www.iuniverse.com


ISBN: 0-595-27347-5


Printed in the United States of America

This work is dedicated to my son Mike, who is even now proudly and ably serving our great nation against all those who seek to do America harm.

# ACKNOWLEDGEMENT

No work of fiction sees the light of day without the faith and influence of good friends and family. I have been blessed with an abundance of inspiration and support from those closest to me in life. I'd like to thank Martha Fitzpatrick, a woman of great refinement and integrity. Without her able and professional assistance the SEAL Strike series would be nothing more than a crazy idea in the mind of an old war horse.

# CHAPTER ONE

A tremendous blast tossed the lead vehicle four feet into the air. The car twisted, coming to rest with a crashing screech of metal on concrete. Despite the car's heavy armor, it was difficult to believe that anyone inside could've possibly survived. The well-hidden attackers drew a steady bead on the last car in line. The rear vehicle in the motorcade popped off the pavement—taking a direct hit through the back windshield. The shot was devastating. The engineer who designed the car's special ballistic glass never intended for it to stop a rocket propelled grenade, or RPG, at point blank range.

The black sedan flipped over on its roof, spinning wildly like a child's toy. The few pedestrians unlucky enough to be close to the attack, scattered in every direction. Two of them, a mother and her daughter, lay motionless on the now bloodstained sidewalk. Chaos reigned on the narrow Columbian street. Suddenly the roar of automatic gunfire erupted from the flat rooftop opposite the smoking motorcade. In the middle of the security convoy sat the last untouched Mercedes, blocked on the narrow street by the other two sedans. It was apparent the heavy machinegun fire was having little effect against the car's armor plating.

Rifle fire cracked through the early morning air. The two Delta Force soldiers were the sole survivors of the RPG attack. They dragged themselves out from under the car, an action made more difficult by its position upside down on the road. The American bodyguards gathered together behind the sedan in an attempt to protect them from the increasing rifle fire.

"They want us to keep our heads down!" shouted the taller of the two soldiers. "They're preparing to rush the precious cargo!"

The term precious cargo was well known among protection teams. It simply referred to the object or person a team was protecting. In this case it was a very important person located in the middle car.

"I think you're right, Sarge!" said the second soldier, a heavily built man in his early thirties. "Should we haul ass to the car?" He pointed with the barrel of his MP-5 submachine gun toward the middle sedan containing the precious cargo.

"No Bill!" called Sergeant Ford. "We need to scoot across the street. Get inside their position. If we're lucky, we can capture that big gun on the roof and turn it back on these goons!"

Bill shifted to place more of his muscular frame behind the burning car. He considered the sergeant's idea for a moment, and then nodded in the affirmative.

"Yeah, you're right, Sarge. We'll just get our ass kicked sitting over there." Bill gestured toward the middle car with his chin. He looked his sergeant in the eyes, his face set in grim determination. "Screw it man! Let's just do this thing, Sarge. Let's just do it!"

Special Forces Sergeant Tom Ford stretched out his hand. Bill took it and squeezed. He knew deep down inside that the odds of surviving were heavily stacked against them. Both men knew it would be a miracle if they could pull this off.

"Okay Bill, let's leapfrog as two fire teams. I'll go first, find a good spot to cover you and then wave you over. We'll aim for that alley right over there." Ford pointed to a gap between two storefronts on the other side of the street.

Bill looked at the alley. He didn't see a better option so he nodded head. "Okay Sarge, make your move! I'll cover you!"

Ford gave his partner a thumbs-up. The Delta men initiated their planned maneuver. Sergeant Ford jumped up. He quickly moved around the trunk of the car and sprinted across the street toward the attackers. For a tall man he moved deceptively fast, weaving back and forth to present a more difficult target. Bill watched the tall army sergeant make his move then opened up. Bill tried to give the sergeant a fighting chance by lying down a withering base of fire with his MP-5 submachine gun. He fired directly at the attacker's rooftop position, spraying bullets all along the edge in an attempt to keep their heads down.

Meanwhile, the M-60 had never ceased firing at the middle car. The continuous rain of lead effectively isolated the vehicle. Anyone trying to approach or exit would be cut in half! The sergeant's sprint across the street did draw the attention of several enemy riflemen. They shifted their aimed fire to prevent Ford from reaching the entrance to the alley. The ambush was only two minutes old but to the Americans fighting to survive, it seemed a lifetime.

Bill changed magazines and got ready to go. Ford had finally reached the other side of the street and crouched down. He caught Bill's attention and calmly waved him across. Bill marveled at the senior man's attitude. Sergeant Ford was definitely a pro. The kind of SF soldier they put on army recruiting posters. Bill just hoped he could measure up to his partner's skill and poise under fire. Bill waved back. He took one last look around to gauge their situation. It was painfully obvious to the Delta man that he and his partner were heavily outgunned and probably doomed to end their lives in this dirty street. His MP-5 was fine for close-in personal security, but this was straight infantry stuff. Oh well, he thought. He wasn't getting any younger.

Bill popped out from behind the car and fired at the roof. He sprinted toward the alley. It seemed like his partner was a mile away. Ford watched Bill take off. He slid his body out and away from the storefront pointing his weapon straight up, drawing a bead on the edge of the roof. The sergeant didn't have an identifiable target but he could pour fire on the building. Their combined efforts appeared to be working as shredded stucco drifted down to the street below. The enemy riflemen ducked down to avoid the hail of bullets from the men of Delta Force. Maybe they stood a chance after all. Nobody was firing back!

Just as Bill made it to the alley a group of guerillas burst onto the scene near the burning lead car. Ford dove back toward the building, diving down and rolling to avoid being hit. Bill stepped into the alley to put the wall between him and a sudden burst of rifle fire. He carefully poked his head around the corner to have a look see. What he saw was his sergeant lying on the pavement without protective cover.

"Hey Sarge! Over here!" Bill yelled, trying to get his partner's attention. Ford didn't answer but instead started to crawl as fast as possible toward Bill.

This was taking too long! Bill was sure Ford would fail to make it to the alley before the guerillas wised up and zeroed in on him with their automatic weapons. He opened fire over the sergeant's head — forcing the bad guys to scramble for cover. Ford came to his feet and sprinted the last few feet, passing Bill and lunging into the empty alley just in time. Bill's MP-5 bolt slammed back and stopped firing. He was out of ammo. Cursing loudly Bill rolled around the corner to join Ford, slapping his last thirty round magazine into the magazine well.

"We did it!" he shouted. Bill was now certain they'd make it the roof. He could see a stairway at the back of the alley leading directly to the top of the store.

"Bill, look out!" Ford's warning was too late. Bill's eyes followed the other soldier's gaze upward to the rooftop. The fragmentation grenades seemed to drift down in slow motion. The two men watched frozen in horror as they realized what was going to happen to them. There were at least seven grenades in the air now. Dropped by the guerillas from the roof above. Both men tried to react but it was too late. Two of the grenades exploded with a devastating blast right at head level. The others made it all the way to the ground before exploding. When it was over the two Americans lay dead.

The three men sitting inside the middle car heard the rapid succession of grenade blasts, unaware the last two American defenders were dead. The smoke was so thick in the street it had been impossible to follow the gun battle outside. They could only listen. During the running gun battle Senior Chief Auger couldn't tell how many of his personal protection team were still engaged with the attackers. The elite navy commando was the body man for the team. His job was to stay in close contact with the precious cargo no matter what happened. He sat there.

Frustrated that he couldn't go outside and help his army brethren. But the senior chief would never leave the car. His place was here with the VIP. To do anything else would be breaking faith with the men fighting outside.

Everyone on the joint special operations protection team expected the others to be professional and do their duty. Auger was the only navy SEAL in the group. Although he was relatively new to the bodyguard business, he certainly wasn't new to the business of being a team player. So he waited. Waited as the Columbian guerillas finished off the last of the Delta soldiers.

Outside, the guerillas swept the kill zone and signaled to the machine gunner to stop firing. The silence was deafening. Auger knew the moment of truth was at hand. He peered through the car's bulletproof window and spotted the guerillas deploying in a defensive circle around the three cars. This was a definite no win situation. Auger's thoughts were interrupted by the sound of men applying explosives to the door of their sedan. Auger turned to the precious cargo, General Mark Alexander, Commander, United States Southern Command.

"Sir, we only have a few seconds before they blow these doors wide open! You have to move to the center of the car, now!"

General Alexander was the four-star in charge of all United States military activity in Central and South America. The theater CINC, or commander-in-chief, was in the process of touring the city of Bogata Columbia to show support for the joint American-Columbian counter-narcotics program. He shot a cold look at his navy bodyguard. He wasn't used to taking orders, especially from sailors. The general grudgingly shifted his body closer to the center in compliance with his bodyguard's request.

"Well, since you're in charge Senior Chief Auger, What do you think they'll do once they get in here?" The general's voice revealed the dread they both felt.

Auger thought before answering. They were both wearing civilian clothes. He looked hard at the older man. The general was in his late forties, gray hair, with a solid build. He really didn't look a day over thirty-eight, and that gave the SEAL an idea.

"Look general, I've got a plan. You and I are about the same size and look nearly the same age. When these guys bust in just play dumb. Don't let on which one of us is the real VIP. You follow me sir?"

The general nervously leaned over to look through Auger's window. He could see the guerillas were scrambling to clear the area around the car. "Alright navy man. But this idea of yours better work. They might not want me alive. They could be trying to kill me you know."

The SEAL looked directly at the senior man and grinned. "Sir, in that case it doesn't matter, we're both toast!"

General Alexander grunted, unconvinced. "Okay SEAL, we'll go with your plan, for now. But what about our ID?"

Auger kicked himself for not thinking of it first. "Good call sir! Give me your wallet, we'll toss it in here." Auger indicated the secret armrest compartment used to store weapons in the Mercedes. The SEAL took both their wallets and dropped them in, slamming the armrest shut. "Carlos! Did you follow all that?"

The driver twisted around in his seat. "Yeah boss, I understand the plan. But somehow I don't think they'll want to kidnap the schmuck driving the car."

Auger's response was violently swept away as the car doors blew off with a loud thunderclap. The explosion was tremendous in the small confines of the limo. All three men dove to the floor of the car to avoid the flying debris. Auger saw Carlos throw up his arms as a man forced himself into the car. Three rapid shots rang out. The sound caused by the automatic weapon was so loud in the small Mercedes that it momentarily stunned the SEAL. Carlos' body was blown back through the now gaping hole where the driver's side door had been moments before.

The general's side door had also been blown open and was hanging by a hinge. He was bleeding from one ear. Auger watched helplessly as the general was yanked roughly from the back seat of the car and thrown roughly to the street. This was it! Auger knew he must survive.

He began the mental process that would give him the best chance to make it out in one piece. The senior chief changed his mindset, going passive. It was best to avoid physical combat and stay alive for now. He hoped the general would have the sense to follow suit.

On the dirty sidewalk the general struggled against the two men holding him. The general thought his size would intimidate the smaller Columbian gunmen. He was wrong. It only served to anger the proud young men. He was thrown violently to the ground and three of them began kicking him as hard as they could. One guerilla stepped up and struck the general a vicious blow to the temple with the butt of his rifle.

A young bearded face pushed itself into Auger's line of sight, blocking his view of the beating. "Venga aqui!" the man shouted angrily in Spanish.

Auger tried to comply by sliding across the seat but apparently wasn't moving fast enough. A rifle barrel slammed into his gut, knocking the wind out of him. He was sure the man had cracked a rib with the blow. He was rudely dragged the rest of the way by two more guerillas. Once out of the car, the SEAL could see General Alexander lying on the street in the fetal position, blows from the angry guerillas raining down on the unconscious man. The man to Auger's right shouted something at him he didn't quite catch. The SEAL turned his head to respond. An explosion of light and pain streaked through the enlisted man's brain, then there was darkness.

## San Diego California–Coronado Beach

Navy Lieutenant Matthew Barrett cursed, staring at the glowing green face of his luminescent dive watch for the third time in the last ten minutes. Damn it! It was thirty minutes past midnight. He was going to be late two nights in a row, and tonight of all nights! Matt knew Tina wouldn't fall asleep. She would wait up for him. Today was the one-year anniversary of their first date. Boy would she be pissed! Matt spun around to study the ground between him and the SEAL training facility a quarter of a mile away straining to spot the truck carrying the oncoming hell week shift. It was too dark to see anything. Damn it was cold! California nights were always chilly.

Matt turned back to address his shift chief, Chief Petty Officer Saunders. "That damn relief crew should've been here half an hour ago! Those bone heads are going to screw up the entire schedule!"

Chief Saunders was always calm and cool. He poured another cup of steaming coffee from his thermos and screwed the cap back on. "Well LT, Chief Jackson's a good man. I can't believe he'd screw us over for the hell of it. There must be a good reason for this delay."

Matt knew the chief was right. He thought of the VHF radio lying on the hood of the gray navy pickup truck. He could always call, but that would broadcast the problem on the command net. The radio conversation would be monitored and eventually the executive officer would learn there had been problems with the shift turnover. Matt decided he couldn't use the radio. He had another thought. Maybe he could drive to the compound and find out what was happening. He knew the shift leader wasn't supposed to leave the BUD/S class. He was the primary person on site responsible for the SEAL students and the ten man instructor staff. But then again, he would only be gone for a few minutes.

"You're probably right, chief. I'm just jumpy because I have big plans after this shift's over. This screw up is kind of cramping my style. If you know what I mean."

"Well sir, we could wait five minutes after you left and then just mosey on over with the class. Just call me on the radio if you need us to bring the class into the compound any sooner. Nobody will be the wiser. They'll just think you planned it that way!"

Matt smiled. What a great idea! "Okay chief, I'm out of here!" Matt grabbed the radio off the truck's hood and jumped into the cab. The truck roared to life. The chief smiled at the lieutenant and waved as Matt backed the vehicle up. Matt waved back and rolled onto the sand road leading back to the training complex.

Every SEAL hell week shift was composed of an officer and a senior enlisted SEAL. Their primary duty was to ride herd on the younger instructors and make sure the schedule was followed without too much deviation. Matt realized he was lucky to have Chief Saunders covering his ass. He pulled off his ball cap and ran a hand through his wavy blond hair. He needed a haircut, bad! The truck was set in four-wheel drive but it still required skill for Matt to stay on the road. He was soon nearing the back gate. Home, sweet home!

Matt had spent the better part of two years assigned to the SEAL training center in Coronado. He had a great job as far as instructor billets went. He was the officer-in-charge of the third and final phase of BUD/S training. Third-phase was the place where the young baby SEALs first learned the art of war. Ground tactics, land navigation and weapons training were a daily staple. Special explosive techniques were also taught to the young tadpoles. All the third-phase instructors loved the schedule.

Matt's instructor staff knew they were the only BUD/S instructors able to maintain their war fighting edge while still on shore duty. Shore duty was two years long. The two years were supposed to be a break between the longer seven-year sea duty tours. The basic underwater SEAL course, or BUD/S, was one of the few shore duty assignments available for the SEAL team officers and sailors. The SEAL instructors at BUD/S were dedicated to their mission. Their mission was to prepare volunteer sailors for eventual duty in the fleet units—the famous navy SEAL teams. During a two-year shore duty tour all officers and enlisted men took turns supporting hell week.

Working hell week wasn't so bad. Matt rather enjoyed the five-day long training process. Watching boys become men and men become SEALs. Nothing much had changed in over twenty-five years. The class attrition rates still hovered around the historical norm of eighty percent. An old saying burned into a wood plaque hung above the entrance to the facility, bluntly summed up the reality of the BUD/S experience. It simply said "the cowards never started, and the weak dropped out along the way".

Matt slowed to a crawl as he drove through the back gate. He saw the trucks of the oncoming shift sitting motionless near the first phase office. They were clearly staged and ready to go but there were no instructors in sight. Matt cursed under his breath and picked up the radio.

"Blue shift chief, this is blue shift OIC." OIC stood for officer-in-charge. The chief's voice responded immediately.

"Roger blue OIC, this is the chief, over."

"Chief, bring the kiddies home. I don't think the group here is leaving anytime soon."

"I'm way ahead of you, blue OIC. I started moving the herd right after you left. They should be there in two minutes."

Matt again was amazed at how navy chiefs seemed to anticipate and make the right call in almost any situation. But then Matt had always been lucky enough to work with great senior enlisted SEALs.

"Roger that, chief. I'll wait until I see them before I go out searching for the oncoming OIC."

"Copy that," the chief said. "Blue chief out!"

Matt sat in the truck considering on his predicament. The hell week shifts rotated in three, eight-hour sessions. The first-phase instructors supervised most of the work in each shift. These professionals knew the drill, understood the evolutions, and were able to extract just the right amount of pain and anguish without stepping over the line. The other second and third-phase instructors like Matt, assisted by covering logistics and safety. They drove trucks, provided medical support, acted as lifeguards, and arranged chow for the students.

In addition to safety, shift officers were responsible for preparing the formal documentation of any incidents, accidents, or student requests to volunteer out of the program. In the late 1990s, the demanding SEAL course underwent intense scrutiny from liberal congressional delegations. Some of the visiting staffers felt the training procedures were antiquated and out of touch with modern and more humane techniques. They strongly believed that it was time for a change at BUD/S. In their opinion politically correct America would no longer tolerate the harsh reality experienced by the SEAL students. Luckily their assault was repelled without inflicting too much damage. Interference did result however in creating a complicated assortment of additional legal paperwork. Paperwork designed solely to cover the navy's ass.

Matt was parked near the student classrooms. Matt could hear the hell week class before he saw them. The forty-nine dog-tired students shuffled into the compound. Each boat crew carried a one hundred and fifty-pound IBS on top of their heads. They moved to an area just to the right of Matt's truck and lowered their black rubber boats. The IBS, or in official navy jargon, the inflatable boat—small was manned by a seven-man student crew. Every boat had an officer assigned as the boat crew leader. The leader/officer sat in the back of the rubber boat, shouting commands to the paddling crewmen and steering with a paddle. The class leader put the class at parade rest with a barely audible command. The students obeyed, feet slightly apart, hands clasped behind their backs.

They all wore kapok life jackets, an oversized bright orange pain in the ass. The canvas straps were routed across the butt and through the crotch, finally attaching to the front of the flotation device. The canvas straps relentlessly sawed back and forth against their inner thigh muscles. The camouflage fatigues worn by the students provided little protection from the abuse. The addition of beach sand made wearing the kapok life jacket a special instrument of torture. The crews of young men stood next to their boats three men to a side. Their officer-coxswain stood in the rear.

By the time Matt got out of the truck some of the students were already falling asleep. Nodding off as their weary heads dropped forward, resting on the padded collar of their kapoks. The sleeping men wobbled a little but found some way to keep from falling down while taking their short catnap. Matt walked briskly toward the first-phase instructor's office. He realized the continuing shift change delay would most likely provide the tired students with an unscheduled sleep period.

Matt walked through the door, ducking to avoid the shiny brass ship's bell, hanging just outside the office. He scanned the room finding it empty. Matt did see daypacks scattered about on the instructor's desks.

This fact indicated that there were instructors in the compound. On a hunch Matt left the office, heading straight for the classroom area.

Matt heard murmuring and laughter. He pulled his jacket sleeve up and checked his watch again. It was twelve forty-nine in the morning. He found the instructor staff engaged in a briefing for the first student evolution of their shift. In the back of the classroom the off-going shift officer was chuckling at something said during the presentation. He spotted Matt coming through the door. His smile faded when he saw the angry shift officer's bloodshot eyes.

The delay really wasn't his fault. He'd been forced by the school's director to wait for the medical team to show up. The Doc and his navy corpsman were supposed to conduct a checkup at two o'clock in the morning, but according to the schedule the students would be too far away for an easy link-up. To make it work the instructors would've had to shuttle the medical team back and forth, adversely impacting the tightly controlled hell week schedule. Lieutenant Junior Grade Smith didn't want to get into a pissing contest with LT Barrett because he really admired the man.

Smith knew Matt Barrett was a recipient of the navy's highest award for courage under fire—the Navy Cross. His combat exploits in Egypt a few years back were also well known in the SEAL community. According to people close to the action, Matthew Barrett led a small team of SEALs into Egypt to conduct a reconnaissance of a critical airport in support of the United States rescue operation. His team's original mission was to look around and report the target's status to the oncoming raid force comprised of Army Rangers.

The Rangers eventually flew in by helicopter to assault the airport but things went to shit. The Ranger force got waxed by Egyptian terrorists using stinger surface to air missiles. As a result of this disaster Barrett was ordered to put his SEALs on target and hold the airport until a second raid force could be assembled and launched. Before it was over, Barrett's eight men had accounted for one hundred and eleven enemy dead. Barrett and his chief, a guy named Auger, were badly wounded but all the SEALs were extracted from the airport without loss of life.

LTJG Smith decided he would be apologetic out of respect. "Hi Matt! Good to see you!"

"Well Dave, great to finally see you too!" Matt said sarcastically. "Why don't we go outside and talk about it!" Matt swept his arm toward the door. LTJG Smith sighed and walked outside. Just outside the door to the classroom was a covered walkway. There was a pipe running horizontally the length of the overhang for the students to use as a pull up bar. The LTJG turned and placed his hands over his head, gripping the pull up bar.

"Matt before you get started, hear me out. The old man told me to stay and police up the medical guys and take them with us in the trucks. We're going to be too far away when the med check is supposed to go down. You know Doc. He takes forever to get his shit together and so we fell behind schedule for the shift change." Before Matt could respond both men heard the sound of shuffling feet.

"Looks like my chief called your chief," observed the oncoming shift officer. Matt nodded in agreement. "I guess they didn't feel like waiting for us cake eaters to finish our cat fight!" Both men laughed. The students were given commands to take off their life jackets. The class leader assembled the students into a long single file line. The tired men followed the student conga line into the classroom for the planned evolution brief.

"Come on, Matt. Let's go back inside and hear the rest of the briefing."

"All right, Dave." Matt responded.

The two SEAL officers followed the last of the students into the classroom. An instructor from the fresh oncoming shift stood by the chalkboard, running his index finger along an elaborate track marked on the board. From all appearances the diagram looked like the board game Candy Land. According to the instructor, the tired students would be all over the base, running and up and down the Coronado beach until dawn. The endurance course required them to walk, run, and even paddle.

The students would move continuously, competing against each other until sunrise for the small favor of a few minutes sleep or a little extra food. With the closing words of the briefing the two shift officers moved away from the door. The instructor shouted the order for the hell week class man their boats and the room exploded with the rumble of scrambling students. Matt and Dave waited for the herd of students to squeeze through the door. Just then they heard the loud and unmistakable clang of a ship's bell. The two officers looked at each other and ran to the first-phase office. They were too late.

The officers arrived as the third and final ring echoed throughout the school's compound. A forlorn looking student stood in front of the first-phase office door, his hand still resting on the fancy rope work hanging from the bell's striker. The young man reached up and pulled off the green helmet liner that signified his status as a first-phase student. The helmet liner was marked in white paint to show his rank and name.

Matt knew what was coming next so he attempted to beat feet. "Is the turnover complete?" Matt asked.

LTJG Smith knew exactly what Matt meant. The officer stuck with this quitter would have a lot of forms to fill out. Smith checked his watch. "Yeah sure Matt. Get your guys out of here. This bone head just created an hour of paperwork for me."

Matt paused. Tina was probably already pissed at him for being late. "Look Dave, why don't you get going? I can handle the report on this quitter. He's really my responsibility anyway since my shift brought him to this."

Dave didn't have to think the proposal over for very long. "Are you sure Matt? I mean if you are, that would be great!"

"Yeah sure, Dave, why not. I'm already in deep shit with Tina. How much more damage can I do being another thirty minutes late!"

"What going on? I thought you two were getting serious."

"Yeah, well she's all into the marriage thing. I don't know what I want. Sometimes I think I'd rather have it simple again. You know, single and free of attachments."

"Well if I can help…"

"No, I'm just whining, Dave. You'd better get rolling buddy."

Dave gave up. "Okay thanks, Matt. I owe you one."

"Bullshit, Dave, you don't owe me anything. You know the deal. We're in this together–teams and shit!"

The LTJG reached out his hand. A guy wearing the Navy Cross could get away with being an asshole. But Matt was truly a good guy.

"You're right on that point, Matt. But I can still say thanks."

With that the ongoing shift leader turned to address the nearest instructor. "Alright boys, let's saddle up!"

It took Matt forty-five minutes to interview the young student who quit. The paperwork was tedious and overly redundant. In the old days if a man rang the bell three times that was it. No post psycho, evaluation stuff. Just goodbye and there's the door! Matt was having a hard time keeping the student awake. The warm office was causing the guy's face and hands to swell. Matt knew that most hell week students reacted this way after being cold and wet for so long.

He directed the man to sign the final document and called in the student duty officer. "Escort this student to the hell week tent and help him collect his personal equipment. Then take him to the duty bunkroom. Make sure the roving patrol checks on his status from time to time until morning."

Matt left the phase office and walked over to the instructor's locker room. He stopped before opening the door and checked the time. Boy was he late! Screw it, he thought. I'll skip the shower and wear my stuff home. That ought to shave a minute or two off my drive to Mission Valley.

Matt could barely stay awake during the long drive back. He pulled his car into the common parking area in front of Tina's townhouse and slowly made his way to the door. Fumbling with his keys, Matt finally entered and quietly walked up the stairs to the bedroom. Tina woke up the second Matt's tired body hit the sheets.

"This isn't working," she groaned softly.

Matt sighed. "Come on, honey, not right now! I'm beat. And besides it wasn't my fault this time."

Tina wasn't buying it. "Matt, it's never your fault! You waltz in here at two thirty in the morning. You never even called to say you'd be late! And to top it all off, you knew I was waiting up for you!"

"Tina, look, I didn't think the shift turnover would take so long. I didn't call because I thought we'd wrap things up and I'd get home on time. You know how these hell week shifts work. We don't call the shots, the students do. I'm sorry you waited so long but it just couldn't be helped!" Matt rolled over and attempted to end the discussion with body language.

Tina wasn't going to let up. "Matt, how can we even think about getting married and building a life together if you can't even honor your commitment to me now? For God's sake Matt, this is only shore duty! What will it be like when you get reassigned to the SEAL teams again?"

Matt knew Tina she was right on that point. She had touched on the only concern he had about their relationship. Married life in the teams was tough. Many active duty SEALs spent over two hundred days a year away from home. They were often unable to tell their wives where they were going or when they would be back. Matt realized too late that he hadn't answered Tina's question fast enough.

"Okay, I get it now. I'm just a convenience. You don't really intend to make this work!"

Matt knew he couldn't win this argument. He was pretty sure he loved Tina but he had his doubts about her ability to deal with his SEAL career. He knew he could always get out of the navy and try to make a go of it on the outside. Tina would love that. But Matt wasn't so sure he'd be happy doing something else.

"Tina please, can't we talk about this after I get some shut eye? It's nearly three o'clock in the morning!"

"Sure Matt," she punched out. "As usual we can always wait until you're ready to talk about it!" Tina pulled the covers tighter around her shoulders and became quiet. Matt smiled. Now he could sleep.

The clock radio read four twenty a.m. when the phone started ringing. Matt snapped out a hand, snatching the handset from the cradle before the second ring. He listened for a few seconds and then groaned. "I don't believe this!"

# CHAPTER TWO

Matt dragged his feet as he walked up the three flights of stairs. He walked along the outside balcony, which ran the length of the staff building. Matt opened the outer door to the director's office. Located in the center of the BUD/S facility, the director's office held a commanding view of the school. The old man was standing by the window when Matt came in, surveying his domain. It certainly wasn't normal working hours so the director's secretary wasn't at her desk. Matt left the door open.

"Come on in, Matt, have a seat."

"Yes sir!" Matt answered.

Matt looked around to make sure there wasn't anybody else there. The presence of other senior officers would indicate he was in some kind of trouble. Or maybe something went wrong and they wanted a statement or something. You never knew what might happen in the navy. Tradition stated that officers in charge were responsible for everything that happened on their watch, even if the officer himself did not do anything wrong. There were all sorts of sad stories about young officers getting nailed. Cutting short their careers.

There wasn't anyone else in the office. Apparently this meeting was for Matt and the director alone. Matt sat down on the short couch adjacent to his desk.

"How ya feeling?" asked the older man.

"Well sir, I'm okay, but I am kind of curious why you had me come back into work. I only just left." Matt couldn't figure out from the tone of the director's voice whether or not in he was in hot water. He decided to be a little less caustic.

"I mean, sir, couldn't it wait until I came back on shift?"

"Matt, I received a SPECAT message an hour and a half ago. I was the only one allowed to go in and sign for it at the message center. I had to drive in from Poway. Do you know how far that is from here?" Matt simply nodded. He was sure the director was about to tear his head off.

"The originator of that classified message was the office of the Joint Chiefs of Staff. The subject of that message was you, lieutenant!"

"Me sir?" Matt murmured. What could possibly be in a special category message for him, Matt thought, the director continued.

"Matt, the message is fairly brief. You're directed to report to the Pentagon in Washington D.C., within twenty-four hours. The message states you are going to be in charge of a special operations team being assembled by the national command authority." The director paused. "Do you have any idea what this might be about?"

"No sir," Matt said. The shock caused by the announcement left him numb. "No sir, I'm attached to BUD/S. You know this is shore duty. I shouldn't be doing any operational stuff!"

The director shook his head in disbelief. "That's right, Matt. I don't know what clown decided to pull one of my instructors out of BUD/S. You and I both know there are plenty of capable officers in the operational SEAL teams on both coasts. Why pick you?"

The director's words were both questioning and accusing. "Your guess is as good as mine, sir. Maybe it's a mistake."

"It might be a mistake but I'm not going to ask if it is or not. Now, Matt, if you get out there and find out this is a mistake of some sort I would appreciate it if you hightail it back here. I'm short two officers as it is!"

"Yes sir," Matt replied. "Will do! Sir, I have one more question."
"Yes?"

Matt continued, "Are you sure the message didn't say anything about the reason for all this?"

"No, son, it didn't. The message was clear and to the point. Lieutenant Matthew Barrett, United States Navy, is to report within twenty-four hours. This message will act as official orders for all military transportation." The director stopped reading and looked at Matt. "That basically gives you a blank check to arrange immediate transportation at any military facility in the United States. Do you need to wrap anything up here before you leave?"

"No sir. I take it I can't tell anyone I'm leaving?"

"You know the deal, Matt. This baby, what ever it is, is code word access only. But I thought you were single. Do you have someone special here who will ask questions if you disappear?"

"Yes sir, well sort of. I live with a lady. She's already pissed about the whole SEAL thing. She'll freak out if I play cloak and dagger with her now. If you would please tell her I had to go to San Clemente Island on an emergency. Say it's a training accident and I was assigned to investigate or something. That will give me a week to sort this JCS thing out."

The director reached out to Matt and shook his hand. "I'll do my best. You need to get your shit together and roll on out of here. Call me if you need me."

Matt returned the firm handshake. "Thanks skipper! I'll let you know when I know."

Matt suddenly remembered a problem. "Sir, there is one thing I am concerned about. I have a heck of a lot of paperwork stacked up on my desk. I saw your request for the quarterly third-phase budget."

Matt was a good officer. Instead of whooping it up about his timely escape from the funny farm, he still had a sense of duty to his SEAL unit.

"Don't worry, Matt," the older man said calmly. "I'll make sure somebody looks at the stuff on your desk, and if you don't get back in time we'll get input from your phase instructors and get the budget worked out."

Matt left the office holding the SPECAT message. He immediately started doing mental inventory. He had his basic combat load in the locker room. It would only take a minute or two to grab his gear. As a third phase instructor Matt spent quite a bit of time patrolling with the students. His personal equipment was squared away as a result. Matt was ready to get going. The old juices were beginning to flow. He had a fleeting image of how Tina would react to all this. Well, Matt thought, he had some thinking to do on that subject. Things might not be the same when he came back.

## The Pentagon-Washington, D.C.

The Chairman of the Joint Chiefs Staff glared across the table at the other service chiefs. "Gentlemen, we need a plan I can show the president! How the hell are we going to get our people back? So far, only the navy has put forth a proposal worth looking at seriously. They of course believe this is a navy special operations job. I see the logic of their argument. Especially since our boys at CIA think the guerillas will take General Alexander and the senior chief to their main sanctuary on the Ariari River."

"Yes sir, the navy believes we have the expertise in this particular situation." The admiral looked up and down the long table to gauge the reaction of his army and marine partners to his comments. "As we stated earlier, sir, the best option is to use a select team of SEALs. As you know these men are uniquely trained to execute operations in this environment. A small team of hand picked SEALs will conduct surveillance of the river encampment, then direct and support the rescue force upon our order."

"Admiral, I'm going to reserve my judgment on the second part of your recommendation. I do agree with your assessment that moving through the jungle would be much tougher to accomplish than coming down that river." The chairman stabbed his finger at the map. "I'm leaning toward a concept consisting of two phases. Phase one, reconnaissance surveillance by the SEALs, and Phase two, the rescue of our people. I want to study the rescue options a bit further. All service assets will be dedicated to support both phases of this operation. Do we have a name for this lash up yet?"

"How about; Operation Green Dagger?" The admiral was in the zone.

"Okay Jake. We'll designate this; Operation Green Dagger. Any other questions? Comments?" The commandant of the Marine Corps raised his hand.

"Yes, sir, I do have a question. I'd like a minute of your time to dispute the navy's logic. I can't believe that it's prudent to allow the SEALs to penetrate so far inland. Sure it's a riverine environment but the corps has a long history of successful operations such as this, and, sir, SEALs are still sailors. Marines can bring more to the table in my opinion. While the SEALs are certainly capable warriors, I believe that the Marine Corps force reconnaissance units are the best team we can field for Operation Green Dagger."

"Of course sir, as you might expect I respectfully disagree with the commandant's conclusions." The admiral looked sideways at his marine counterpart and maintained eye contact. "If I may, chairman, I'd like to bring out a few salient points that my esteemed associate may be unaware of and, therefore, overlooked."

"Go ahead, Jake, but make it brief!" The chairman checked his watch. He was late for a meeting with the national security advisor.

"Yes, sir, thank you! First and foremost, we have predefined levels of expertise in this area. Marine force reconnaissance units are second tier forces. They are very effective in a conventional sense. Sir, I mean no disrespect to the commandant or the corps, but I do not recommend we send in a second tier force to conduct a first tier level mission. Sir, in addition I respectfully suggest you compare the actual credentials, capabilities, and training expertise of a four to five man SEAL surveillance team, and a force reconnaissance unit. While both are made up of patriotic American men, the SEAL's ability to communicate and send back real-time photography and video stream using state of the art equipment far outclasses any conventional tier two unit the Marine Corps could put on the ground."

"Any other thoughts?" the chairman asked, looking around the room. He focused on the marine four-star across the table. None of the chiefs felt like jumping in. "All right then. I concur with the logic of using tier

one SEAL elements. It's a riverine environment and as far as I'm concerned riverine means water! The marines are a superior military unit
when directly pursuing their own conventional mission but this case is
clearly different. This is a strategic event. And I might add, a politically
charged event. The SEALs are far better for this type of thing." The
chairman turned to address the admiral. "Quite frankly, Jake, if you guys
pick the right men you should be able to pull this off.

"I'm way ahead of you, sir. I took the liberty of recalling a potential
mission commander, Lieutenant Matt Barrett. He led the SEAL platoon
that pulled off that miracle in Egypt a few years ago. He's steady as a
rock!"

"All right, admiral, I'll leave phase one of Operation Green Dagger in
your capable hands." The chairman took one last look around. "Unless
any of you have any objections in this matter, I will adjourn this meeting. No? Good! Jake, I expect the draft operations order on my desk
within twenty-four hours."

With that said, the chairman stood up. The chiefs all rose to their feet
and remained standing until he departed the room. "Good job Jake!"
The commandant said without looking at the admiral.

"Sorry, Pete. It's the same old game. Whoever goes to the show gets all
the dough." The commandant nodded. He knew that traditionally the
Marine Corps always received the smallest budget of all the armed services. He was also aware that whenever a real world mission was conducted it was, then, used as justification by the different services to sell
their need for more money to support that mission area in the future.
Fighting for mission assignment was really a funding battle in disguise.
Being assigned a real world strategic mission by the national command
authority was like winning a new multi-million dollar contract.

"No problem, Jake." The commandant replied. "You have an operations order to write. Do you need any help?" Jake smiled. "You bet, Pete,
I appreciate all the help you can give me." Both men buried the hatchet
and got to work. In the end they were Americans first.

## Medellin, Columbia

Pablo Chavez stood on a pure white balcony overlooking the city. He quietly smoked one of the fine cigars from his collection. He was tall for a Latino, still in good shape from twice weekly racket ball sessions. Chavez was a handsome man with the high fine facial bones of his Spanish ancestors. He was one of the richest men in the world, and yet, he knew something was missing. Gone was the thrill of the early days, when running coca leaf and protecting his jungle processing plants filled his hours with danger and the promise of personal combat. Chavez wasn't the smartest businessman ever to ply the coca trade but he was the most ruthless.

Month after month, Chavez would roam the deep green jungle of Columbia like a conquering general. He'd identify, and then eliminate the production facilities of his dwindling competition. His operations in turn were protected by Columbian guerillas in a devil's pact. In time, the guerillas grew to depend on the funding source. This unholy alliance allowed Chavez to roam freely throughout Columbia, safe from his enemies and from the government. Any official who asked too many questions about Chavez's activities soon wound up dead. The Americans, helping the Columbian government in their fight against the drug trade, wanted Chavez for multiple arrest warrants, but they continued to come up empty-handed.

Few knew that Chavez's main purpose in traveling abroad was to organize his financing and distribution channels in Europe and Asia. Chavez owned vast estates in at least five countries. His record keeping was meticulous. He trusted no one to do this mundane task, preferring to do the work himself. He conducted himself as a legitimate businessman in each of these countries.

All the proceeds from his coca trade were laundered several times through various banks. Chavez used a sophisticated computer software program that made it virtually impossible to trace any of the dollars back to him. Chavez hired top money management people and investment advisors to place the laundered money into various world stock markets. He also increased his wealth by buying selected distressed real estate in third world countries.

It was safe to say Chavez was making as much in income from these other endeavors as he was from the original coca trade that made him his first million. But all this only served to take the zip out of his life. His semi-retirement had seemed a death sentence. Then the Americans changed his life forever. The primary architect of their campaign was the general in command of U.S. Southern Command stationed in Panama. General Alexander worked effectively to coordinate the efforts of the Columbian military and police. Venezuelan efforts along the shared border with Columbia worked hand-in-hand with the United States Special operations units to deftly cut off the flow of coca.

At first it was all a nuisance. Another muted attempt by the Americans to capture a few headlines in the war against drugs. But never before had the Americans persisted for so long. Never before had the Americans used their special operations and intelligence capabilities to such great effect. Chavez soon realized the Americans were out to ruin him. If he waited much longer without taking action his entire coca business would be destroyed. The Americans were difficult to bribe, unlike the Columbian military.

He could probably bribe a few low-level players, maybe assassinate one or two of the American leaders, but it really wouldn't matter much in the end. If the Americans really wanted to stop the coca trade they could do it. Chavez and his top lieutenants had decided that the best way to make America stop their attacks was to make it more painful for them to continue those attacks. Americans had always been susceptible to the taking of hostages. The American people wanted their people back at any cost. They were willing to give almost anything to avoid international humiliation.

What better target than the architect of his problems than General Alexander of the United States Southern Command. Chavez himself hand picked the operatives to conduct the attack and kidnapping. A few well-placed bribes here and there, kept the local police well clear of the city streets the day of the ambush. The ensuing firefight had been more deadly and prolonged than Chavez had thought possible. The body-guards had turned out to be Delta Force soldiers and a SEAL. The American bodyguards were unwilling to die easy. Out of the twenty-man team sent in, Chavez lost twelve. Two or three of the survivors were severely wounded and recovering.

Chavez left the balcony and walked into his sitting room. Now the Americans would understand a price must be paid if they messed with him. He was determined to stop them and extract his revenge.

## The Columbian Jungle

Senior Chief Auger was thrown violently to the ground. The air whooshed out of his lungs and he struggled to breathe. The men around him laughed and began to kick Auger repeatedly, screaming obscenities in Spanish. He knew he had to get up quickly or they would start break-ing ribs. His hands were still tied behind his back. Auger struggled to roll over until he was face down on the ground. He scooted back until he was at last resting on his knees, forehead pressed into the hard dirt. The attack did not abate. One of the Columbian guerillas began slapping his rifle barrel across the navy man's back.

Stand up! Auger mind screamed the command. The senior chief ignored a particularly brutal blow and pressed himself into an upright kneeling position. He ducked a wild stroke aimed at his head and jumped to his feet. Standing, his full height intimidated the smaller men. The Columbians backed off a few steps, assessing the situation. They gave him enough room, showing respect for his size, and indicated he should walk around to the front of the truck. Auger could barely see around the rusty vehicle. There was a small group of guerillas, four or five at most, gathered near the front of the truck. Auger took muster. Counting the two or three goons having fun with him, there were a total of six to seven armed men.

Auger quickly assessed the situation. He was in the deep jungle, pos-sibly hundreds of miles from any town or city. Even in his battered condition a dash through the jungle might work, but then what? He took stock of his captors. The guerillas seemed very relaxed, even comfortable. That usually meant that they were on home turf. You could also count on plenty of friends operating in the area. No, he would bide his time. Wait until there was a clear opening, an opportunity to escape. Auger knew help would be on the way soon enough. The powers that be would be cranking up the machine. Committing satellite time and attention on this area of the world. These guys had to have camps, training areas and such. American eyes in the sky could detect thermal signatures emitted by fires and even humans. As long as Auger kept his head, he had a fighting chance to make it out of this scrape alive.

The SEAL scanned the immediate area for a sign the general was traveling with him. He seemed to remember there had been another crate in the back of the truck but nothing moved inside during the long ride. His attention was refocused on his plight with a sharp jab to the ribs. The small smiling man was having loads of fun, prodding the big American with his rifle barrel. His concerns about the general were soon put to rest. He was pushed rudely onto the jungle trail. The path took an immediate turn to the right and there was General Alexander.

The general was surrounded by a new group of guerillas. He seemed okay. At the very least he was alive. The new group of guerillas were older, more seasoned. Auger's escorts conducted a brief exchange of responsibility and returned to the truck.

"So you must be the country folk!" The senior chief's quip was answered with a sharp rap to the head. I'd better cool it, Auger thought. A few more hits like that and I won't be able to balance my checkbook anymore. On cue, two men lifted the stretcher holding the general. The old man moaned. Maybe he's been sedated, guessed Auger. The senior chief remembered that just before the goons knocked him out, the general had received one hell of a beating.

"Venga! Venga!" The insistent voice belonged to a grizzled-old coot, urging Auger to start walking while pointing an old bolt-action rifle at Auger. His coal black eyes spoke volumes, reflecting the harsh life he'd led. Auger nodded ever so slightly in deference to the old man and did as he was told. The group moved out. The patrol wasn't in any hurry Auger noted. They moved at a casual pace. Conserving their strength. Auger recognized the indications immediately. He was in for a long trek.

The men weaved back and forth, trading off stretcher-bearers from time to time. The jungle was so thick that it reached out and touched you. The heavy air was stifling. It was very difficult for Auger to breathe. Chief Auger looked up. Maybe his hope the satellites could find them, was misplaced. The triple canopy of vivid green blocked any possible view of the sky. Hopefully the truck's movement and heat signature was sufficient indication that people were doing strange things on the ground. Auger knew the spooks back at the national security agency were experts at recognizing routine activity so they could pinpoint things or activities that were unique and therefore subject to further investigation.

The senior chief's stomach growled loud enough for a guerilla to show he'd heard. Man I'm hungry, he thought. I wonder if these guys are planning on ever feeding me. Then again, maybe they don't want to waste food on a man marked for death. The initial confusion over who was the actual VIP would, most likely, be resolved when they reached their destination. Auger walked all day without a break. Twice the guerillas gave him water. His strength was returning and he began to consider the possibility of escape. Based on the size of the canvas back-packs the guerillas carried, they could be on this patrol for two or three days before arriving at their main base camp. Maybe he could slip away at night. Find help somehow. Or make a statement before dying, tied up like a hog. It would be great to get a hold of one of those weapons, take a few of them with him. Auger knew his fantasy was silly. He'd have to stick with the general. Auger absentmindedly wondered if anyone back home was on top of this problem.

# *The Pentagon, Washington, DC*

Matt shuffled his feet uneasily in the waiting room. This was his first visit to the Pentagon. Although he'd felt intimidated at first, the more he looked around the more he realized it was nothing more than a huge office building. Many senior officers from the various services were moving about the hallways, scurrying up and down the stairwells. Most were not in very good shape. A fact that confirmed Matt's assessment that he was in the world of the staff pukes. Top-heavy paper pushers trying to rule the military kingdom from a desk, without getting their hands dirty.

Matt still wasn't sure why he was there. His orders had been clear as mud. Upon his arrival he spent an hour at the main entry point. The staff personnel at the check-in desk were appropriately impressed with the origin of the orders but were as confused as Matt as to their meaning. They eventually sent Matt to the JCS conference room. A tall army colonel greeted him.

"Lieutenant Barrett?" he asked.

"Yes sir," Matt replied. "I was told to…"

The colonel interrupted Matt, extending his hand. "My name is Colonel Troutman. Please be patient, you will soon know more than you really want to know." Colonel Troutman reinforced his mysterious comment with a wink. The colonel stepped aside and held the door open. Matt was ushered into what appeared to be a small briefing room. Three men were sitting around a conference table. None of the men stood up to shake Matt's hand. One of the men, a navy admiral, pointed to a chair.

"Please take a seat, Lieutenant." Matt couldn't stop staring at all the fruit salad on his chest. Each colored ribbon represented a different military award, and the four stars on the admiral's collar were certainly impressive. Matt spotted an elaborate badge positioned just under the man's breast pocket. It suddenly dawned on him he was sitting across from the Chief of Naval Operations.

The man to the CNO's right was wearing a suit. He was in his early fifties with a touch of gray at the temples. He had that air of authority that comes with access to the top, the untouchables. The man oozed arrogance from every pore. Matt was sure this schmuck was CIA or maybe even NSA. He decided then and there that he disliked the man. At the end of the table sat a gentleman Matt recognized immediately. The Chairman of the Joint Chiefs of Staff.

"Welcome Lieutenant Barrett, I trust your trip from San Diego was pleasant?"

Matt betrayed himself by swallowing hard before answering.

"Yes, sir, thank you sir."

The chairman began with introductions. "Mr. Barrett, this is Mr. Collins the assistant to the director of operations for the CIA." The suit stared back at Matt before offering his hand. Great, Matt thought. Some insecure idiot that wants to play head games. Matt returned the handshake and then promptly ignored him. The chairman took all this in before introducing the admiral.

"This is the Chief of Naval Operations, Admiral Jackson." Matt smiled and shook the offered hand.

"It's nice to see the navy here sir." Matt wanted the admiral to know he might need an ally. Matt turned his attention back to the chairman. "Please excuse me, sir, if I appear a little confused."

"That's understandable Mr. Barrett." The chairman slid a plain yellow eight by ten envelope across the table towards Matt. "Lieutenant, the contents of that folder will explain some of the issues we are going to be dealing with during the pre-mission planning phase for Operation Green Dagger. We have two Americans in jeopardy, lieutenant. They have been taken hostage and we presume they are being moved as we speak to a large base camp south of Bogotá, Columbia. You will find the details and background information in the envelope. All our intelligence resources are at your disposal."

Matt wasn't getting it. "Sir, what does this have to do with me? I'm assigned as an instructor in our special warfare center."

"Son, you have been selected by the navy to lead a very special team. Initially, the team will be responsible for conducting reconnaissance and surveillance of the guerilla base camp in question. The camp is located smack dab on a river in the Columbian jungle. You and your fellow SEALs have been tasked with helping find and rescue General Alexander, Commander, U.S. Southern Command and one of his SEAL bodyguards." That got Matt's attention.

"Who's the SEAL, sir?"

"Actually I believe you know him." Matt's heart sank.

The chairman continued. "His name is Senior Chief Auger. I understand you two worked together at one time."

Matt couldn't believe it. "Auger? Are you sure, sir?"

The chairman didn't change his expression. "That's right, son. All we know right now is the Columbian guerillas ambushed a vehicle convoy in Bogotá and took General Alexander and your friend. We tracked the bastards by satellite. They drove into the jungle and we lost contact with them. Lieutenant we don't have much time. You need to pick the rest of your team and assemble them in Panama. We have people coming in to brief you on the events that led up to the hostage taking. They will also make sure you have all the information you need to plan and execute your mission."

The chairman looked at the bank of clocks on the wall. "You have less than seventy–two hours to assemble and brief your team. Spend a few minutes after this meeting and sketch out your immediate logistics needs so we can get that ball rolling. Remember Lieutenant Barrett, if you are able to locate the hostages you will then transition to rescue support. Do you have any questions about the objectives this operation?"

Matt shook his head. "No sir, I think I've got it down. You want me to go in and find these bastards and see if our people are still alive. If they're there and alive, you want me to tag the site and provide support on the ground for a follow-on rescue team."

"That's exactly right, lieutenant. You were chosen to lead the way on this operation because of your combat experience and because you proved you can think under pressure. Your actions in Egypt are proof of that. Good officers, the ones that know how to lead men, are rare, even in special operations. Pick your team wisely. You need to pull this off right the first time." The chairman stood up to leave.

Matt jumped to his feet. "Yes sir. You can count on that. I know just the men for this job and it won't take long to put the team together."

"Good, that's no less than I expected," the chairman said. "Admiral I concur with your decision regarding Barrett. He'll do a good job! I wish we had more like him!" The chairman left the room, followed by the spook and Admiral Jackson. Colonel Troutman spoke up.

"Matt, take a moment to review the material in the envelope. It's enough to get you started. If you know whom you want on this mission give me the names now. I'll chase them down and send them to Howard Air Force base in Panama ASAP!"

Matt barely heard the colonel.

# CHAPTER THREE

## Fort Pickett, Virginia

The gloved hand gently pushed the branch aside. The SEAL sniper shifted his weight ever so slowly, adjusting his field of vision. He now had a clear shot. The target area was a simulated urban compound. A training site referred to as a MOUT facility. The acronym MOUT stood for mobile operations in urban terrain. Various scenarios could be set up to help train U.S. military forces deal with the difficult task of fighting in a city environment. The SEAL sniper was laying in wait assisted by another SEAL who acted as security. They were one of four sniper pairs that encircled the MOUT facility.

The SEALs were about to attack the simulated town. The sniper's mission was to identify the exact location of two American pilots held prisoner. Then the main assault force would swoop in and rescue the two men. They were conducting the raid in broad daylight so the SEAL Team Four training department could videotape their actions on the objective. Video cameras were positioned throughout the MOUT area and inside the rooms occupied by the opposition force and prisoners. The opposition force consisted of reserve army personnel. They knew their job was to die but they planned to make it as difficult as possible for the SEAL rescue team.

The SEAL snipers were also required to demonstrate their marksmanship skills for the training department's graders. Upon hearing the execution code word over the secure radio net, the four sniper pairs would fire on the exposed sentries. When the snipers initiated fire the rescue team would blow the doors and windows with special explosives to gain access into the key building. During the fight the sharp shooters were tasked with killing any enemy threats attempting to leave or reinforce the primary building.

But for now, the men hidden around the town provided up-to-date intelligence information to the over all mission commander. The command and control element were positioned on a hill next to the town. From this vantage point, the SEAL commander could observe the evolving attack and orchestrate solutions to problems as they arose. The mission commander was assisted in his efforts by two SEALs, a radioman and a rifleman responsible for the element's security. Code words and critical information flowed back and forth via scrambled VHF radios. From time to time the radioman passed the information updates along in the form of intelligence reports to the SEAL platoon's boss circling high overhead in a supporting air force AC-130 gun ship.

During the mission-planning phase, the SEALs were provided with critical information from national intelligence sources. The key piece of the puzzle pinpointed the location of two American hostages. They were being held in the second story of the hotel near the center of town. The SEAL sniper had already visually confirmed this report. There were terrorists on two or three of the rooftops in the immediate vicinity of the hotel armed with Russian AK-47s assault rifles. Petty Officer First Class Sam Oberman, sniper, could see a man on the nearest rooftop scanning intently with binoculars. The man focused most of his attention toward Oby's position, unaware of the danger lurking in the tree line.

"What time is it?" Oby didn't want to take his eyes from the scope.

Petty Officer Third Class Donaldson used a pair of high-powered German binoculars to scan the entire target area. "Two minutes to eight. I can't see the assault team, Oby. I hope they're in position by now!"

"The assault team is coming through the sewer," Oby explained. "They should be entering the side street, coming up through the manhole covers right around now."

Donaldson knew the plan. The rescue team was going to stage themselves next to the target building sixty seconds prior to the assault. If everything went according to the rehearsal, at exactly eight o'clock the demolitions breaching team would lead the SEALs as they rushed across the open space between the back alley and the hotel. Upon their arrival, the demolitions team would place a special wall-breaching package on the side of the target building. Small hand-held shields protected the breechers from the blast. The explosion would create a six-foot high by four-foot wide hole in the cinder block wall. The breechers then needed to get out of the way while the assault team sprinted into the smoking hole.

"Yeah Oby, I know how it's supposed to go down," the young scout said. "I just wish I could see they were in position."

Oby snorted. "Did you ever stop to think that if we could see them, the bad guys could see them? Don't worry about the assault team. They know what to do. Just focus on helping me identify secondary targets once the shooting starts. What time is it now?"

"Forty-five seconds to execute." Donaldson's voice was all business now. Oby was right. Each SEAL was responsible for his own actions. BUD/S taught you that. The team was well briefed, well rehearsed, and well led. It was up to Murphy now, he thought. Murphy's Law stated that if anything can go wrong, it will go wrong. In special operations, it was wise to say a small prayer to Murphy to hedge your bets.

Of course mistakes were bound to happen. The two SEALs had witnessed quite a few during complex exercises like this one. Then again, that's why they practiced all the time. There is no such thing as a perfect mission when you pushed the performance envelope every training day. Most SEALs believed a perfectly executed exercise was a waste of training time, since nobody learned anything when nothing went wrong.

Donaldson swept his binoculars back toward the target building. "Thirty seconds, Oby."

"Roger that!" acknowledged the sniper. "Watch for the assault team popping up."

"There they are!" The scout could see a line of men snaking around a building adjacent to the target. He shifted his view to the rooftop sentries. "Everything's still cool topside! Ten seconds to execute."

Oby pushed the selector switch to the FIRE position. "Heads up," he whispered. The scout didn't respond. Oby inhaled fully then slowly let air escape from his lungs. He stopped halfway through the exhalation and held his breath. Oby began squeezing the trigger.

BOOM! The breeching charge detonated two seconds late. The explosion was greatly amplified due to the many empty cinder block buildings in the town. Oby didn't wait to confirm he'd nailed the first of four mannequins representing the terrorist snipers. Oby smoothly shifted his cross hairs, resting on the head a second sentry dummy. The weapon jumped in his hands. This time he saw the head explode.

"Topside targets waxed!" Donaldson scanned the windows and then looked at the base of the building. "No secondary targets in sight, Oby!"

Oby didn't answer. He shifted his scope to each window on the target building, methodically moving from window to window. Donaldson was correct. He couldn't find any new targets to shoot. He kept his eyes on the windows anyway. The dumb shits always wanted to come out and take a look. Sure enough, a mannequin's head slid slowly into view, just high enough for Oby to take a shot. These training guys are great! It was tough to set up a training evolution where all the players participated fully. Oby took the shot. The Mannequin flipped back out of sight.

Nobody paid attention to the shattering glass and sounds of struggle emanating from the hotel. Everything was going according to plan. After the assault team entered the building, they quickly secured the ground floor. Meanwhile the other sniper pairs were executing their tasks. Dropping all the exterior targets in their field of view. The assault team killed two more terrorists as they ran up the stairway toward the second floor. In the first fifteen seconds of the assault the SEALs eliminated eleven terrorists, a very respectable body count considering none of the SEALs were yet killed or wounded.

Oby heard the assault team firing a rapid series of shots as they cleared the second floor. "How's it look?" he asked.

"Still clear everywhere I can see," responded the scout. "Our kill zone is empty. There are no visible targets!"

The firing suddenly increased dramatically. "Sounds like they found the hostages," observed Donaldson.

"Yep," remarked Oby. "Unless those crafty training guys set a trap for our boys over there."

Donaldson lowered the binoculars. "You really think so, Oby? That would suck big time!"

Oby continued the sweep the cross hairs of his high-powered scope back and forth, looking for fresh targets. "I was on an assault last year and they fed us bullshit about the hostage location in the building. We went charging in there and started clearing the rooms one by one until we hit the third floor. The training department had a wall of desks and chairs built in the hallway. Every time we tried to take it down they opened up on us."

"So what did you guys do?" Donaldson said, placing the binoculars back in front of his eyes.

"We sent a six man team up the stairs to the fourth floor. They cleared that deck and used ropes to lower themselves down to the third floor windows. They tossed in a few flash crash grenades and came in through the windows shooting. We had the floor,
    but no hostages."

"They weren't on the third floor?" Donaldson was having a hard time keeping up.

"No, they weren't," Oby continued. "The training guys moved them just before the attack. They moved them through a sewer access door in the basement of the target building. It took a while but we found them tied up alone in the building next door!"

"Man, that is bullshit!" Donaldson had less experience then his sniper partner but he'd been a SEAL long enough to know how the game was supposed to be played. The hostages were always in a bad position when a team came in hard, fast, and in broad daylight. During such a dynamic entry and assault there was nothing to stop the terrorists from putting a round in their hostages just out of spite. The SEALs counted on violence of action to overcome even a prepared enemy.

"Violence of action" was a tactical concept crucial to the success of small unconventional units. It meant never letting the other guy have the drop on you. Hit him first and hit him hard. Never give him a chance to fight back. The bottom line was simple. It was far better for a small team of SEALs to go in and eliminate the bad guys in their sleep, rather than call them out on the street like an old western to determine who had the fastest gun. Any biker in a bar fight knows the concept called violence of action works. In a bar fight, if you start to shove and talk trash to a seasoned street fighter, they'll just hit you over the head with a stool in mid-sentence.

Immediate escalation of violence is so shocking and so unexpected that virtually every opponent falls victim to the tactic. Applying violence of action to hostage rescue scenarios entailed using the rude impact of shock and precision firepower, in a coordinated and deliberate fashion. Ideally that put shooters everywhere at once. The element of surprise wasn't always enough. You had to get the other guy to stop and wonder what was going on. Make him blink. Then it was much easier to take that guy out of the equation.

The earpiece crackled to life in Oby's ear. "Stand down, the exercise is complete. All players muster at the target building's main entrance."

"Roger that," Oby said immediately. "It's quitting time buddy!" Oby started packing the equipment staged around him.

"That's cool," Donaldson commented. "Because I desperately need to get a big ass ten-legged bug outta my shorts!" Oby laughed.

The assault team brought the rescued hostages downstairs to the main entrance. The team leader was on the radio net, methodically sending out a detailed status report to the command and control element. They, in turn, passed the report to higher authority circling above. If this exercise had continued normally, the assault team would've gathered in all the sniper and breeching teams to patrol to an off target helicopter extraction site.

The preferred formation shape for travel was an oval. The hostages moved in the middle, protected on all sides by members of the assault team. The team leader moved right behind this core group. The command

and control element up on the hill over looking the target area would've packed up their radios and raced to the helicopter landing zone, arriving ahead of the main body. The extraction birds would then be called in to take the SEALs and hostages to a safe zone. Today's exercise however was different, focusing only on actions in the objective area. The training staff intended to only debrief the attack and rescue sequence.

Oby and Donaldson slid backwards out of their firing position and threw their heavy packs over their backs. The two SEALs walked down the steep hill toward the MOUT facility. SEALs were flowing into the center of town from all around. The SEALs called this "going admin." The term was also used to taunt a fellow SEAL who cheated or cut corners during training exercises.

"Oby!" Oby recognized the voice of SEAL Team Four's training officer. This couldn't be part of the exercise. The training officer wouldn't be using Oby's name over an open radio net like this.

"Roger, this is Oby," Oby replied.

"Oby, you and Donaldson get down here ASAP! I need to talk to you. I have a priority message from the commanding officer for you. I already told the team leader and mission commander that you aren't going to be with them for the final head count."

Oby was puzzled by all the cloak and dagger stuff. "Whatever you say boss," he replied, pressing the talk button on his small radio.

"What's up?" Donaldson could see Oby was troubled.

"Don't know. They said the old man sent me a message. Mr. Jackson says it's important. We need to find him down there. He said to ignore the team muster."

"That's weird!' Donaldson observed. "Are you in some kinda trouble?"

"Not that I know of," said Oby. "I guess we'll find out when we get into town." The two SEALs picked their way through the thick underbrush. At times both men cursed the tangle of vines and dead plant life. Eventually they broke into the open, clearing the tree line forty yards from the muster point. Oby spotted Lieutenant Jackson over near the corner of the target building. The officer waved at the sniper team.

The training department was diligently moving about, cleaning up grenade canisters and spent brass. Some of the instructors headed upstairs to dismantle the barricade in front of the hostage room on the second floor. Still others were picking up the pieces of shattered cinder block where the breeching team blew the wall. The grease used to stick the charge against the door had splattered the wall with black goop. The SEALs were responsible for cleaning up any mess made in the army's training facility. Soon, an army range control sergeant would arrive to clear the MOUT and certify it clean and ready for use by the next unit.

Oby and Donaldson walked over to where Lieutenant Jackson stood waiting. "So what's up boss?" Oby asked closing the distance. "Well Oby," the lieutenant started. "It seems you've received special orders back at Little Creek." Oby stopped dead in his tracks.

"Special orders?" he asked. "I thought I was in trouble!"

"No Oby, you're not in trouble. The orders were SPECAT. Nobody but the old man and you can look at them. I've told the team you'll head right back to the creek and go straight to the captain's office."

"If it's SPECAT it's real world shit!" Donaldson blurted out. Oby thought for a moment.

"I need to take my long gun, sir. Especially if it's the real deal." All snipers were issued five different specialized weapons. Oby's other weapons were in the team armory in Little Creek.

"Fine, Oby, you do that. But promise me you'll get your butt on the road right away. My ass will be in a sling if you don't show up soon."

Oby stuck out his hand. "Sure thing, sir, I'm moving as we speak." Oby shook hands with Donaldson and said a quick goodbye. A waiting pickup truck, driver at the ready, was idling nearby. Oby jogged to the truck, threw his gear in the back and jumped in the front seat. He hid his rifle by covering it with a poncho somebody left in the cab. Oby's heart was pounding as the truck pulled away from the MOUT area. Real world missions were the reason all SEALs trained with such intensity. He was pumped!

## Stuttgart, Germany

Petty Officer First class, Boone Kilpatrick shook his head. These guys can't draw a straight line, he thought. Boone was temporarily assigned to the naval special warfare unit in Stuttgart as a reconnaissance instructor. His home command, SEAL Team Two in Little Creek, Virginia, was asked to provide a man with experience in reconnaissance and surveillance. His job for the time being was to teach some of the newer SEALs the fine art of target sketching. Boone wasn't the greatest artist himself. But he could draw a straight line. He could also write neatly and legibly. A critical skill if you're making maps and charts for someone else to use.

The five SEALs in the classroom seemed incapable of grasping both requirements. "This exercise is simple gentlemen," he began the lecture for a second time. "All you have to do is duplicate the drawing I've placed on the chalkboard. By duplicating the drawing neatly enough for someone else to read, you're halfway to being real recon artists!" Boone didn't believe a word of it. As if to punctuate the end of Boone's sentence, one of the SEALs in the back dropped his pencil. His head bobbed and his body jerked around as he struggled to escape the confines of the small student desk in pursuit of the writing implement.

This is a waste of time, Boone thought. None of these guys want to be a point man let alone part of a surveillance team. What I have here is a couple of M-60 machine gunners, a couple of demolition guys and a buck toothed ensign. Why are they even in this class? Why did they send me over here? Boone walked to the front of the classroom and checked his watch for the hundredth time.

"All right guys, we only have five more minutes before we're through for the day. All that I ask is that you finish this drawing so we can move on to the rest of the curriculum tomorrow." The five-minute warning seemed to perk up the class. The SEALs frantically worked to finish the drawing assignment now that they knew the end was so close at hand.

The door to the classroom opened a crack, the rusty hinges complaining loudly. Boone heard the sound and looked at the source. One of the administrative naval personnel for the unit was standing in the doorway holding a note. He beckoned to Boone to come over to the door. Boone glanced at the class. They were all scribbling away. Boone walked over and grabbed the piece of paper handed to him. It was a memo from the unit's operations officer. Boone raised his eyebrows. The note said he was being ordered to Panama! Panama? SEAL Team Two was responsible for Europe and the western Mediterranean. Panama was SEAL Team Four's area of operations.

"Hey Boone! Can we get out of here now?" Boone nodded without looking up from the note. He stepped aside absentmindedly as the students bolted for the door. Why Panama? Boone left the classroom and walked rapidly toward the OPS office. This has to be a mistake!

## Somewhere in the jungles of Columbia

Auger was suffocating. The knotted tee shirt used to gag him was pulled so tightly up against his nose he could barely draw a breath. One of the guerillas was actually sitting on his body, which didn't help matters any. After two days of slogging it through the jungle, the guerillas had linked up with a new group. The newcomers numbered around nine shooters. They looked different somehow, younger. Oh great, he thought. Now we're going to have training classes out here in the jungle.

At sunset, the entire guerilla force assembled on the trail. Auger was roughly hauled up a low ridge to a position ten yards back from the trail. From what little he could see, the senior chief believed he was watching a class in ambush techniques. He recognized the site for what it was, a perfect ambush position. The guerillas gagged the SEAL again and shoved him down to the ground. His best friend assumed the position sitting on Auger's back. The hours crawled by. His legs and hands were numb and the side of his face was on fire from the pressure of being pressed into the small stones and rocks on the jungle floor. He knew something was up when he felt the man shift nervously on top of him. Auger heard the classic sounds of preparation. Sliding bolts, shifting bodies, all up and down the firing line men were getting ready for combat, and Auger was face down in the dirt.

What a bunch of amateurs he thought. Two or three SEALs could kick all their asses. He spent the next few minutes detailing how he would set up the ambush. Claymore mines on the flanks and one back behind the team for rear security. Add in machineguns, forty-millimeter grenade launchers, and the world's best riflemen and all you needed was a target. A SEAL ambush was a real thing of beauty.

His fantasy was interrupted by the sound of crunching of boots coming down the trail. Heavy feet. Tired men at the end of a long walk. Auger knew they would all be dead soon. Tired men are careless men. The trainees were going to have a good night.

The narrow jungle trail made a tight hairpin turn, jutting away from them like an upside down letter V. The ambush position was contoured the same way. They could wait until the target group was bent around the trail and then hit half the group on each side of the V. In the SEAL's opinion, the guerillas weren't using their firepower effectively. The guerillas should be on the other side of the hairpin curve. That way their fire would be focused into the kill zone not split and pointing in opposite directions. Of course Auger was rooting for the ambush victims. If they won maybe they could help the general and Auger catch a cab.

A shattering blast of light and rapid firing signaled the initiation of the ambush. The guerillas were rocking and rolling. Everybody was firing on full automatic. Burning up ammo at an incredible rate. Auger knew what came next. All of a sudden the firing died down. The dummies were all reloading at the same time! The man on top of Auger was spraying bullets in earnest. The hot brass casings sprinkled down on Auger. A few made their way down the collar of his shirt. Auger was now very awake!

Everybody was firing and people were shouting in Spanish but nothing seemed to change one way or the other for a minute or so. Then the pace of firing petered out. A few grenades were thrown here and there, but it was time to clean up and count bodies. The ambush had taken forever. A sloppy mess Auger thought. A bunch of third-phase BUD/S students could do better! The last shots rang out and then silence. A flurry of excited commands, were shouted in Spanish, resulting in hectic activity all along the trail. It looked to Auger like the students were being sent to sweep the kill zone. Almost immediately, firing broke out on the trail. The students were learning that good site selection was more than picking a stretch of trail and sitting down to wait.

The students were discovering the opposite side of the trail slanted downward, allowing many of the ambushed soldiers to hit the ground and roll immediately to safety. With the ridge protecting them, the soldiers were free to run or wait for the sweep team to expose themselves. The first student who stepped on the trail found out the hard way. Two soldiers hiding below blasted him off his feet. The veteran fighters yelled for the students to hit the ground. The wiser guerillas rolled six or seven grenades over the ridge. A few more grenades and a few shots later it was all over.

Senior Chief Auger was jerked to his feet. His legs were asleep and he promptly collapsed. Falling heavily, he pitched over and hit the ground with his face. The guerilla cursed and kicked him. When Auger failed to react the man struck him with the butt end of his rifle. The American stayed low and moved close to the Columbian's feet, making it hard for the guerilla to use his gun as a club again. Auger's legs were screaming in pain as the blood rushed back into tissue. He was lifted to his feet once again by another man who sent Auger's swim buddy off to do something else. His new handler was stronger. He had little problem guiding Auger through the dense jungle to the trail a few yards away.

Senior Chief Auger was placed on the trail next to a large man with gray hair. General Alexander! Both men were alive and uninjured. The general sneaked a quick look at the navy SEAL. His face was covered with dried blood and dirt but his smile spoke volumes. They were both still in the game!

## SEAL Team Three–Coronado California

Lieutenant Jared Stone, platoon commander of charlie platoon, SEAL Team Three, reported to his commanding officer's office as ordered. He'd been pushing paper work for hours, having just finished a training trip to the California desert. Charlie platoon was the team's designated hostage rescue platoon. They were especially adept at taking down ships and oilrigs. The platoon's primary responsibility was to be prepared to respond immediately to fleet command directives.

Stone wasn't sure why he'd been called to the captain's office, but he assumed that one of his men had gotten in trouble. That meant an ass-chewing. Captain O'Connor gestured through his opened door for Stone to enter.

"Morning, captain." Stone decided to act cool and calm.

"Morning Stone, have a seat." Captain O'Connor indicated he wanted Jared to sit on the plush couch against the wall. As the lieutenant sat down he couldn't help but see the old man's professional history splashed on every wall in the room, plaques, flags, other mementos of all kinds. Memories of the teams and experiences Captain O'Connor cherished. Someday, Jared thought, I'll have all this. Someday I might even be captain of my own SEAL team. The captain was ignoring Jared. A minute or two passed until O'Connor finished up a short stack of paper work. Next to him on the large desk was another stack twice as high.

On second thought, maybe I don't want this job. Jared hated paperwork of any kind. The captain finally stroked the last signature and looked up. He leaned back in his plush executive chair. "Son, your platoon is being placed on a high state of alert. This is a real world, national command authority directive. You will be going to San Clemente Island were you will be placed in isolation. I don't know much about this whole thing, yet, but I do know your platoon has been designated as a support asset for a highly classified rescue operation. This should be right up your alley."

"Sir, will I receive a tasking order or intelligence package to work from?" Stone was starting to get excited.

"As I said lieutenant, I don't know much yet, but I will push to get you what you need!"

"Yes, sir, I understand." Jared really didn't understand but that was okay. He was going on a real mission!

"Some aspects of the general mission scenario will be fed to you while you're in isolation out at the island. Remember, isolation is just what it sounds like. No contact between your platoon and the rest of the world. Take all you standard hostage rescue equipment and basic load out, but don't neglect to take your heavier weapons. This could turn out to be a long patrol. If that's the case, you don't want to get stuck with only sub-machineguns."

"I see," Jared said. "Sir, my platoon's still in the compound. We returned from the desert two hours ago. Can I pull them together real quick? I'm afraid the chief might start cutting them loose to go home."

"Yeah, right. Go ahead. I think this is a good deal for you, Jared. Keep your guys straight, practice and work on your skills out there so when the time comes you are sharp." The older man stood up. "Security classification is top secret. No one else in the team is to know the nature of your mission or even where you're going for isolation."

Stone was ready. "Yes sir!" he said jumping to his feet. "Excuse me, but is that all, Captain?" The captain smiled. He was jealous of the young lieutenant. He wished he were still young enough to lead a SEAL platoon. He'd never had a chance to go into combat. He just missed Vietnam and was getting his graduate degree when Operation Desert Storm went down. Stone was a good man. He'd get the job done and bring his SEAL platoon back in one piece.

"Get out of here, son, and good luck!" The SEAL captain extended his hand. Jared shook his captain's hand, pumping maybe a little too vigorously.

"Thanks sir, we won't let you down!" Jared turned and left the office. Man, oh man, he thought. The boys are going to shit!

# CHAPTER FOUR

## *Howard Air Force Base–Panama*

Matt shifted his weight to his left foot hoping to provide relief for his right one. He and Boone had been standing on the flight line for over an hour. The burning tarmac toasted their feet without mercy. Matt messed around with the buttons on his navy issue dive watch. He mumbled a curse as he tried unsuccessfully to set the watch to show the correct time in Panama. Boone watched amused as his boss fumbled around with the stupid watch.

"I'll just do the math in my head LT, those watches are too tough for me to figure out, and besides, I liked it better when you only had to pull the stem out and presto the time changed!" Boone was a computer fanatic. Back in the states, he spent hours every night surfing the Internet. He considered himself fairly well versed in the demands of the high tech age, but those dive watches were something else all together.

"You're right, I suppose," said Matt, shielding his eyes with his hand. He looked up and stared into the sun. "It just seems like every time I come to an air base to pick someone up, the damn plane is late!" Matt continued to scan the sky. Boone spotted the plane first. A tiny speck visible just above the horizon.

"Look right over there, LT!" Boone pointed at the small object looming larger and larger as it approached Howard Air Force Base.

"That's it!" Matt said, a little too loudly. "That's the C-9 passenger plane coming in on final approach." He was tired. Matt had hardly slept since the night of his last hell week shift. He traced Boone's outstretched hand to the navy aircraft. "Boone, we need to hurry up and get Oby's shit into the vehicle as soon as the plane arrives."

"You got it, LT! Are we going to tell him what's going on?"

"No, we'll wait until we get back to the secure area. I'm sure he'll understand." Matt and Boone knew operational security was a critical element in the success of every special operations mission. Oby would know the score soon enough. It took forever for the C-9 to taxi down the long runway. It turned eventually onto a smaller taxiway, rolling to an abrupt stop just short of the debarkation port. The air force ground support personnel scrambled to place blocks behind the wheels and get the mobile stairway in place. The engines were shut down with a final groan and the door behind the cockpit opened.

Oby stepped out squinting into the blazing Panamanian sun. He was dog-tired from the flight and from the hectic running around back in the states. "I'm never going to get used to this shit," he mumbled. The seasoned SEAL sniper shielded his eyes and looked down.

"Hey Oby!" Boone shouted over the sound of ground vehicles whipping around the aircraft. He waved energetically at Oby drawing his attention.

"That you, Boone?" Oby shouted back. Oby's face lit up. It had been two years since he'd last seen the lanky point man. He waved back.

"You're damn right it is!" Boone answered back. "The LT's sick and tired of waiting for your sorry ass! I had to bribe him so he'd stay!" Oby started down the stairs, chuckling to himself. It was great to know there were guys you could trust and there was no substitute for old war buddies. Matt had to add his two cents worth.

"That's right sniper man! I was about to go find me a marine long gunner!" Oby arrived at the bottom of the debarkation stairs. He took two long steps and offered his hand to the navy lieutenant.

"Now LT, you know you'd only end up carrying the guy! There is only one great SEAL shootist." Matt laughed, returning the handshake. Boone stepped forward and slapped Oby on the back. They shook hands vigorously.

The three men stood for a moment sheepishly looking at each other. Strong emotions swirled around under the surface. Emotions that could only truly be shared by men who had fought and bled in combat together.

"It's good to see you again big guy, it's been a while," said Matt. Oby looked fit and trim. The past couple of years spent at SEAL Team Four had clearly matured him. He seemed poised and confident. Not the young pup Matt remembered.

"Good to see you guys too!" Oby said. "So, what the hell is going on? They wouldn't tell me shit back at the team area. " Oby lowered his voice, this was no place for a conference.

Matt glanced at Boone, then back to Oby. "We'll fill you in later Oby. This isn't a good time to bring you up to speed." Matt looked around to emphasize the lack of privacy.

Boone nodded in agreement. "That's right old buddy one thing is for sure though, we 're going to be butt deep in spent brass on this one!" In SEAL lingo that meant a mission with a high likelihood of direct combat. "Boone my man, it's time to get down and dirty again."

"Like Egypt?" Oby asked, referring to their shared combat experience two years earlier.

"I certainly hope not," quipped Matt. "Come on, let's grab your shit and get the hell out of here!" Boone smacked Oby on the back for the third or fourth time since seeing him and picked up his partner's daypack. Matt led the way back to their vehicle staged nearby. Boone followed close behind still unable to wipe the smile from his face.

It took another thirty minutes to retrieve the rest of the sniper's operational equipment from the belly of the C-9. Once all the gear was loaded the three SEALs jumped into the navy van and left the airport. The trip from Howard Air Force Base to Rodman Naval Station was a short one. Twenty minutes later the SEALs pulled into what had once been the old special warfare building.

Three rectangular cargo containers stood empty in the parking lot. Matt drove over to the first of the three and parked the van. "All right guys we'll be storing the equipment here in these ready boxes. Use the one on the left for your personal stuff. The other two are for weapons and ammo."

"Your still not going to tell me what is going on, huh boss?" Oby asked.

"All in due time, Oby," Matt replied. "All in due time. I'd rather give you the pitch at one sitting rather than bits and pieces."

Boone couldn't help himself. "I've already got this whole gig figured out."

"Oh Yeah?" Matt replied sarcastically.

"Yeah!" Boone fired back. "This is how I figure it. The President of the United States has decided that some asshole down south needs to learn some new manners. Of course when he turned to his experts and asked for the very best the country had to offer, our names naturally came to mind."

"The president no less!" Matt kept shifting equipment around to make room for Oby's bags.

"Yeah the big guy!" said Boone, without skipping a beat. "Of course once we've completed the mission we'll all be given the Congressional Medal of Honor, free homes, and never have to pay taxes again!"

"Hey Boone, you got an agent? You're a natural if you ever start writing screenplays!" Oby and Boone realized nobody was going to learn anything until the LT was good and ready.

Boone wasn't ready to quit just yet. "No Oby, I ain't got an agent. But come to think of it, that wouldn't be a bad idea. I have a feeling about this one. Probably make a good book. Like you say, maybe even a movie!"

Matt and Oby both laughed. "Yeah in your dreams man!" Oby taunted.

"I don't think you'll be seeing a movie deal any time soon!" Matt said, piling on. It felt good to be back together again. The three SEALs finished the task of storing Oby's equipment in the containers and returned to the van. They drove through the center of the small base and within minutes arrived at the barracks. The three of them would bunk here together. Matt had requested that he be placed in the enlisted facility to simplify their logistics. SEALs were SEALs.

The lieutenant checked his watch. "All right guys, we have an hour before we leave for the army facility at Fort Amador. The big boys want us to be on time for the initial intelligence briefing in the tunnel. From now no speculation, no idle chitchat. We're only going to talk about the operation in secure areas from now on." Oby and Boone nodded in understanding. It was time to tighten up. Their faces reflected a grim determination to do the job right.

## Fort Amador–Panama

Matt, Boone, and Oby sat in uncomfortable gray metal chairs deep inside the secure army's intelligence briefing area known as the tunnel. A short, balding colonel stood near the front of the room. He began the general intelligence briefing by covering the weather in the operational area. Matt, Boone, and Oby stared at the detailed topographic map of central Columbia. This was a standard briefing. The green suits always started with the big picture and the soft information like weather. The afternoon wore on as the experts trooped through one by one. Each briefer provided the SEALs with general and specific information directly related to their mission tasking. At long last they began to discuss the meat of the mission. The final briefing pair, wearing wire rim glasses, entered the room. These were the target analysis guys.

Throughout the proceedings, the SEALs sat quietly. Absorbing the fire hose blast of data. They took time every so often to jot down critical details. Details they wouldn't commit to memory such as assigned call signs, frequencies, and vital ground coordinates. The focus of their activity would be in the triple canopy jungle south of Bogotá, Columbia. The SEALs felt comfortable about the environment and the support involved. It was time to get down to brass tacks. A raw boned Special Forces major stood up and moved to the front of the briefing room. This is it, Matt thought.

"Gentlemen," the major began. "Your mission, by order of the President of the United States and the national command authority, is to conduct a surveillance and reconnaissance operation along the Ariari river basin south of Candilojas, Columbia. This area is controlled by Columbian guerillas and the Columbian cocaine cartel. As you may remember from earlier briefings today, their symbiotic relationship gives these two groups plenty of reason to work together against any outside intruder."

The major reached out to pull a sheet of paper off the easel. "Gentlemen, the purpose of your surveillance and reconnaissance is to determine the location of General Alexander, Commander, U.S. Southern Command, and a Senior Chief Auger, a SEAL. Both were kidnapped during a premeditated ambush in Bogotá one week ago."

Oby and Boone were stunned. Senior Chief Auger was a prisoner? It'd been two years since the mission in Egypt and the breakup of their reconnaissance platoon. In time, they had all received orders to other SEAL teams. None of the old platoon members maintained contact with each other after that so they were unaware that Senior Chief Auger had moved on to join the personal security detachment tasked with protecting high visibility VIPs as they moved around the southern command's area of authority.

Matt turned off the mental images of the senior chief and tried to focus on the major's words. As he spoke, the army officer pointed to the wall map, his finger touching an area colored blue. This area, according to the major, was completely controlled by Columbian guerillas and had been for over ten years. The major strongly emphasized the danger of operating in this zone of guerilla control.

"Men, despite our best efforts, and those of the Columbian government, the guerillas remain in control and have survived all efforts to eradicate them." Matt knew with the cocaine cartel pumping money and weapons to the guerillas, the Columbian army was probably out gunned and even more likely bribed into indifference.

The major finished his mission-tasking brief and relinquished the podium to a tall, handsome gray-haired gentleman wearing a five hundred dollar suit.

"Here it comes," Matt whispered to Boone. "You can never trust these guys!" Boone nodded without answering. The newcomer introduced himself as Mr. Simmons. He appeared very confident, sure of himself in an alien environment. A good chance this guy has military experience Matt thought to himself.

"We have fresh reports of ambush activity ten kilometers from the river. This activity is very close to where we think the guerilla-operating base is located. National intelligence assets utilizing state of the art thermal imaging show a rather large area of human activity on the Ariari River right here." The smooth talking CIA man pointed to the river on the map. "We believe the hostages are being taken to this base."

Boone had a question. "Sir, why don't we just grab them now if we know so much?"

"Son, we believe there's a very high probability the guerillas would execute them if we go in there with guns blazing!" Boone understood the dilemma. The U.S. couldn't resolve this crisis with a great demonstration of power. They needed to be patient. The major returned to the podium. "The security council is convinced the guerillas will use the stronghold to keep the prisoners secure until negotiations can be entered into with the United States. You three men are to infiltrate the area of the primary base camp. Once there you will observe and report on any and all camp activity. We need to know the number of enemy troops. Is there any anti-air capability in the camp? And if possible, ascertain whether or not the hostages are at that location."

Oby raised his hand. "Yes?" replied the major.

"Well sir," Oby began. "I understand what you want us to do, but maybe I'm missing something. Are you saying this is only a look-see operation? I mean, sir, if they are there, shouldn't we try to grab'em?" Oby's question floated out there in the open for a second or two. Matt had been thinking the same thing. Why jeopardize the lives of more

Americans? Why find the hostages and not do anything about it? So far none of the briefers had mentioned anything about rescue.

The major paused before answering Oby's question. "Actually you and your team are restricted in this matter. Your job's to only report what you see. Under no circumstances are you to attempt a rescue. I'm sure you'd agree that three SEALs, while they may be a match for most forces they engage, would be stretched pretty thin attempting to rescue somebody from this camp! Consider also your very limited firepower and the very real possibility the hostages may be wounded and unable to travel.

If you must know there is a rescue team in isolation. They will execute the mission if, and only if, you three are successful in finding the hostages."

Oby didn't buy the pitch, but he was too smart to show it. "I understand, sir. I just wanted to make sure there was a rescue being planned." Oby's stare communicated what everyone there in uniform already knew. You couldn't trust the spooks from CIA or NSA. The civilian nervously glanced at the major avoiding eye contact with the SEAL sniper.

The three SEALs wouldn't say it out loud. But to see Senior Chief Auger, their friend and comrade, sitting as a hostage within reach, and not do anything about it? That didn't sit right with them. Professionally, they agreed with the major's observations. If the hostages were injured, three SEALs would never be able to pull them out. Matt wanted to close the loop.

"Let me get this straight just so everybody's on the same sheet of music. You want the three of us to go in, find this base camp, and report on all the activity in the base camp. I'm assuming you want real-time information flow."

"That's correct," said the major. Matt continued, "Then you want us to feed answers to a pre-selected rescue team so they can come in and save the hostages." The civilian nodded in agreement. Good the SEALs weren't going to cause a problem. He was seemingly more at ease now.

"Yes, lieutenant, that's exactly what we want you to do. Whether or not you stay as the point element for the rescue force will be decided based on the needs of the rescue team commander. Do any of you have more questions on your mission tasking or the immediate area of the target?"

Boone, Oby, and Matt looked at each other. Matt answered for the SEALs. "No sir, I think we have a handle on it. Is there a secure area available where we can start planning this mission?"

The major looked at the CIA representative to see if there was anything else on the agenda. The civilian shook his head without speaking. The major then made eye contact with Matt. "Lieutenant Barrett you and your men can use the secure area down the hall, room forty-seven. All the materials you'll need, maps, etc., have been set up in there for you. Information about the logistics of your infiltration is also available in a workbook marked "mobility". Most of the normal SEAL options for infiltration have been listed and all available mobility assets in theater are also listed in the book in case you want to try something new."

"Yes sir!" Matt was focused at last. He knew Boone and Oby were eager to start working the problem sets. The major continued, "Once you determine how you want to get in we'll set up the logistics timeline. We'd like your team to infiltrate within forty-eight hours and begin sending out reports within seventy-two hours from right now."

Seventy-two hours until show time? Matt considered the time crunch for a moment. Forty-eight hours to plan, twenty-four hours to get in and find the target. They were a little rusty working together but most of the procedures would be straight recon SOPs from the old days. Matt looked up at the major. "That's no problem, sir. We'll go ahead and start working on this ASAP. Sir, if you don't mind, can you arrange to have some pizza or something sent to the secure planning room? We've pretty much been on the go since early this morning."

The major chuckled. "I got it, lieutenant. Do you men have a preference?"

Boone chimed right in. "As long as it doesn't have anchovies, I don't give a shit, sir!" The tension was at last broken as everybody joined in the laughter. Matt had the last word.

"Great, then it is done. Oby, Boone, lets get rolling!"


## Chavez's Private Residence–Mexico City

Chavez paced back and forth in the small foyer. He was temporarily residing in one of his many homes. An exquisite high-rise penthouse residence, kept for convenience sake to conduct business in Mexico City. He peeked at his watch in nervous anticipation that at any second the doorbell would ring, announcing the arrival of his expected visitor. Chavez walked briskly back into the main greeting area adjacent to the parlor, ignoring the well appointed surroundings. An interior decorator had worked hard to give the space a sense of regal splendor, and it'd worked. A place, properly befitting a man of Chavez's wealth and social stature.

Chavez halted his pacing to study the row of photographs sitting on a low ornate table. The pictures where beautifully appointed in silver frames. The people in the photographs were his family. His pretty wife Reza who never complained about the traveling and lack of privacy in his life, and his wonderful daughter. His daughter was safely away from his world, excelling as a second year student at Harvard University in the United States. Finally there was his firstborn child, his son Estaban. Chavez found it very hard to look at his son's image without succumbing to a rush of painful emotions.

Two long years, two years since his son's death. Two years since the light of Chavez's life was extinguished from the face of the earth by the Columbian military under the leadership of the Americans. Chavez had sought revenge against the various pilots involved in the air strike, discretely using personal funds and contacts within the Columbian military to get the job done. But he didn't stop there. He'd also made sure the families of the pilots paid the ultimate price for his son's death.

Chavez looked for answers. His sources informed him that members of the United States military had orchestrated the entire strike. American Special Forces, operating in coordination with the Columbian armed forces. Their objective had been simple. Stamp out the guerillas and the source of their funding, the cocaine cartel, Chavez's own coca operation.

The attacks against Chavez were masterminded by one man, General Alexander. Somewhere in Panama the general and his murderous staff had plotted the demise of Chavez and his guerilla support. The general didn't pull the trigger of the gun that murdered his son. But he did plan the air attack. Chavez now believed that a blood feud existed between himself and the American.

Even now Chavez's master plan was in motion. First, grab the Commander of the U.S. Southern Command. Make the Americans initially believe it was a random act perpetrated upon them by the guerillas. Second, a much more subtle operation, Chavez was going to have his guerillas demand a false ransom request. Requiring the United States to engage in meaningless negotiations. Meanwhile, Chavez's agents were positioning themselves in the United States to kill the families of the American soldiers involved in the planning of the air strike that killed his son.

If all went well, Chavez would end the drama personally. Finally experiencing his final act of vengeance. General Alexander would never see the United States again. A loud rapping interrupted his train of thought. The large brass knocker on the front door signaled his expected visitor had at last arrived. Chavez went to the door, opening it to reveal a man waiting in the hallway. Chavez waved the man into his home. A brief exchange took place. Chavez thanked the man, handing him a small business card. Encoded in the address and phone number of the business card was an account number for a Swiss bank. Funds had been deposited in the visitor's name. Payment for a job well done. Now, Chavez thought, it's time to set the rest of my plan in motion.

# CHAPTER FIVE

## Guerilla River Base Camp–Columbia

Senior Chief Auger tripped over a root and fell down on his face. His legs were throbbing and twitching uncontrollably. They had stopped near a clearing in the jungle. All around him guerillas chattered excitedly. Auger rolled over on his right side to see what all the fuss was about. Below he could see men purposefully working. They were well organized and seemed focused on their tasks. The SEAL realized with relief that their journey was over at last. They had arrived at the guerilla's main base camp.

The river camp was certainly impressive. The cleared area in the center sloped gently down toward the riverbank. The jungle hid more of the camp. The vegetation on the camp's perimeter had been cleared of the first two levels of canopy. This left the tallest trees intact to provide overhead protection from aerial observation. Down by the shoreline two felled trees reached out into the river. It was obvious to Auger the guerillas were using the two huge trees as a makeshift pier. Ten or so dugout canoes were tied to the trees. A cluster of five to six men, were even now unloading weapons and supplies.

The camp appeared to be managed efficiently. Auger noticed guerillas pitching in to assist with various tasks with little or no direct supervision. These people have a strong sense of purpose, he thought. They're not a bunch of bums trying to escape responsibilities of life in the cities. Senior Chief Auger felt the first sting of despair. It would be very difficult to fool these people.

Auger's thoughts were interrupted by a loud thud. A shouted complaint in English confirmed the identity of the man thrown down to the ground next to Auger. It appeared the general was still alive. "I'm happy to find you safe and sound, my friend!" the senior chief spoke in a whisper.

"Ah, yes, my young traveling partner, how are you holding up?" The general's voice was firm.

"So far, so good. I've checked the camp out and I think we'll have a tough time breaking out of here."

General Alexander noted the pessimism in Auger's tone. "More bodies, means more activity. More heat. Finding this place will be a piece of cake for the NSA boys. I think it's best we just sit tight and try to survive this place until the cavalry rides in to save us."

Auger never had an opportunity to answer. The kick struck him square in the back of the head. Sparks shot out in Auger's brain as he struggled to maintain consciousness. The general received his share of physical abuse delivered violently by two of the men guarding them. They yelled at the Americans to stop talking as they stomped and struck the defenseless men.

The beating went on for a few minutes. Somewhere along the way Auger passed out. When he did come around again his head and face throbbed with pain. Ants and small insects crawled in and around his ears and eyes. He attempted to blow them off his face, but that just pissed them off. He tried to zone out a bit. He focused instead on more pleasant thoughts, memories of his time in the teams. He thought fondly of his fellow classmates who went through the world's toughest commando training side-by-side, with him. He fondly remembered the men who helped him get through hell week with a strong hand here or an encouraging word there.

He'd met his wife toward the end of training. A wonderful woman, she'd sacrificed a good career as an executive pilot to marry Auger. She endured his tours of duty and no notice alerts, adoring her navy husband. Their marriage had been unique in the teams. Unique because it survived much longer than any SEAL operator had a right to expect. He realized the threat to his morale inherent in dwelling on his failed marriage. He knew this but still he couldn't stop the flow of feelings and pictures. Yeah, he thought, it'd been a perfect marriage, a true love match. But, in time, the days away took their toll. She became bitter and resentful of the navy, and especially the teams.

Their emotional separation grew until she started to seek the company of others. Sure, she put on a good show whenever they were together, so Auger never realized what was going on behind his back, whenever he left on a trip. After two years of lying and intrigue, his wife confessed to him she wanted out. His reaction had been passive, very professional. Fine, he'd said. You're not happy being married to a SEAL and I don't know how to do anything else. Ironically they parted friends. And from what he understood, she never married the other man in her life. She did however go back to her career. According to Auger's sources, she was now happy and successful. Well, shit happens!

Senior Chief Auger's thoughts were interrupted by the sound of crunching boots. His attention was brought swiftly back to the present unpleasant situation. A harsh voice barked a command in Spanish, demanding that Auger do something. The SEAL didn't have a clue what the man wanted. He stared up at the young man from his spot on the ground. The guerilla was in his early twenties, smooth faced, trying hard to make an impression but failing to pull it off. Not a hardened jungle warrior, Auger thought, probably a recent recruit from the city. He guessed the man had been in the jungle five, maybe six months at most.

The Guerilla waved his weapon around getting more agitated by the minute. He yelled at Auger for the third or fourth time. Auger shook his head and tried to show by his expression that hadn't a clue what the guerilla wanted. The man's response was swift. Auger winced in pain as the young man kicked him violently in the ribs. The SEAL rolled back and forth, trying to avoid the full impact of the blows and show by his body language that he was incapable of following any command. The Columbian suddenly got the picture. Recognizing his error, he reached down and grabbed Senior Chief Auger by the ropes wrapped around his wrists together and pulled him to his feet.

Auger stood up and then went back down to his knees. His legs were numb and half asleep. His right shoulder started throbbing harder. There was a good possibility he'd dislocated it somewhere during the long trek in the jungle. The young man gently helped the American to his feet. He held Auger in place for a moment until the SEAL acknowledged by nodding his head that he was ready to stand on his own. The Columbian's eyes expressed compassion. He released Auger and stepped back, resuming the role of guard.

Auger heard grunts and hard slaps coming from behind him. The general was also receiving his wake up call. The senior chief took another measured step. He turned ever so slightly to steal a peek at the general. His brother captive looked a lot worse than Auger felt. He realized General Alexander must have put up a fight some where along the way. The right side of the older American's face was swollen and discolored. His right eye was completely closed, blood crusting over an old wound on his forehead.

Auger was smacked across the shoulder blades with a rifle and pushed toward the camp. Auger put one foot in front of the other, the blood returning to the muscles in his legs caused a raging, burning sensation. The escorts pushed and prodded the two Americans slightly left and then right arriving at last on top of a small hill near the river. They struggled up the moderate incline until they stood on top at last. Auger and General Alexander stood there staring at the two small cages constructed of crate parts and tree branches.

"Well, general, I guess we should feel lucky it's not a firing squad!" Auger's voice was shaky from fatigue. His attempt at humor sounded hollow. General Alexander stood next to Auger watching the guerillas work out the guard routine.

"What do you think they have planned for us, senior chief?" As bad as the general looked he sounded a hell of a lot better than Auger. Auger realized he'd started to feel sorry for himself. He silently vowed to follow the old man's example and suck it up.

"Well, sir, they aren't going to kill us, I'm pretty sure about that. They went to a lot of trouble to keep us alive and bring us here." Auger's logic was self-evident. The guerillas had only recently built the two cages. From the very beginning of their long jungle trek the objective had been to keep the Americans alive for this, their new home away from home.

"Hostages then? Are we to be pawns in a great game of bodies for bucks?"

"Yes, sir, I think you hit the nail on the head," Auger agreed. "But I think they want more than just money. Maybe something from the United States—changes in our foreign policy or something like that. They don't kidnap a general as important as you for just money."

One of the guards pivoted sharply instructing the two Americans to stop talking. The order was made clearer when he pointed his rifle at Auger. They got the message. Auger took advantage of the silence by checking out his immediate environment. He could see just about everything from the hilltop. That also meant everybody in camp could see the prisoners. No dead space, no cover or concealment if by chance the general and Auger escaped the two cages.

The door of the first cage was opened and Auger was directed to go inside. He had to crawl on his hands and knees to enter the small four-foot by four-foot enclosure. There was barely enough room for Auger's body. He had to curl up in the fetal position pulling his knees up to his chest in order to fit. He watched through the slats in his new home as the guerillas jammed the general into the other cage.

The senior chief took inventory. During navy escape and evasion school he thought the whole fake prisoner drill was pretty much a joke. All SEALs and navy pilots attended the rugged SERE course. Fresh from their BUD/S experience, most SEAL students in SERE School were able to slide right through. The rough handling and verbal abuse was silly after what they had experienced at BUD/S. Not so for the navy pilots. For them SERE school was a traumatic and often life changing experience. SERE school was a reality check. A harsh demonstration, only a demonstration of what a prisoner of war goes through trying to survive.

Cold, heat, sleep deprivation, lack of food, all conspire to break a man down. Even the simple act of standing perfectly still can eventually cause pain and anxiety. All of these were experiences were endured in SERE school. The difference between SERE school and the real thing, Auger was beginning to realize, was that in SERE school you knew they weren't going to kill you. The school played games. This, the senior chief understood all too clearly, was no game.

## Naval Special Warfare Command–Coronado, California

Admiral Fitzpatrick pounded his desk. "Why the hell didn't we send the ready platoon? Who came up the crazy idea that picking a couple of guys out of a hat?" he demanded angrily. "I don't understand how someone in the Pentagon got involved in the first place! They pick the job, I pick the mission team! Whatever happened to standing operating procedures? Whatever happened to recalling standing units? Can somebody give me an answer?"

Commander Witte quietly stood his ground in the face of the admiral's tirade. "Look admiral, I know I'm the plans officer, but this came down from the big boys. You know that I, of all people, understand your frustration. I'm the operations officer for the whole SEAL community. I've spent an incredible amount of time and resources preparing SEAL platoons on both the east and West Coast for war. Testing them. Rating and ranking the various platoons. We put the best on alert status. Those men sacrifice their personal lives by being a beeper call away from war. Sir, I have no idea why the national command authority decided to circumvent that process. But I can tell you every team captain, every officer, chief and enlisted SEAL will think our whole system of readiness is a farce."

Admiral Fitzpatrick raised his hand, signaling the commander to be quiet. "Steve, please sit down." The admiral had calmed a bit while listening to the commander's speech. "Look, Steve, you don't have to lecture me about what should've happened. I know what should have happened. And I don't have to remind you that the national command authority has the right to do whatever they damn well please. But three guys? The teams are going to get one hell of a black eye if this ad hoc group goes down to Columbia and screws up! Of course if and when that occurs, nobody will care if I whine that I had no control over the selection of these men. This is still the United States Navy and I will be held accountable! Now Steve, I want you to focus on damage control. How can we regain control of the operation? I want to know how we're going to cover our ass when this thing falls apart."

Commander Witte studied the floor for a moment. "Well admiral, one thing we could do is look into the records of these men. If we can find any problems or flaws, we can be prepared to prove they were poor choices. In essence, sir, you could tell the national command authority it failed because we didn't have a say in the decision."

The admiral pondered the comment for a moment. "Commander, I don't think you'll find anything derogatory in the records of these men. I've taken the liberty of checking up on them myself. The officer they've chosen, Matthew Barrett, is a holder of the Navy Cross. The other two gentlemen are eminently qualified and are both holders of the Silver Star medal for valor under fire. I don't think attacking the choice of these men is the answer."

"Well admiral, if I could inject one or two points. I've looked into their records and at least in the case of the officer, Lieutenant Barrett. He was a very poor student in BUD/S, sir. His record shows he barely met the minimum standards to graduate. He also nearly flunked out of SDV minisub school. As a matter of fact, he was placed on probation at SDV team two because they believed he was a substandard officer."

The admiral straightened up. "Drop it commander! These men have graduate degrees in combat leadership and you're sitting here rambling about their grade school record. I don't think your idea holds water. No, we have to come up with some other angle to protect ourselves. I want another SEAL platoon put in isolation. I want them training around the clock as a backup team if they have to go in and take over this recon mission. I want this in my back pocket, Steve. I'll try to pull some strings and get the navy to push for a SEAL rescue force. I think it'll fly considering the navy's got a first team going in already."

The commander knew when to quit and go with the flow. You didn't rise to higher rank in the navy by arguing with admirals. "Alright sir, I'll get a platoon up and running. I'll put them in isolation to preserve operational security. San Clemente ought to due nicely. The third-phase BUD/S students left the island last week. The airstrip next to the camp will work as a pickup point for the platoon when it deploys south."

The admiral moved to the window. From his office he could see down the Coronado beach. He could also see the West Coast team compounds and the BUD/S facility. "Make it happen, Steve. Do it fast! The pace of this mission scenario could pick up without warning."

"I'm on my way admiral!" Commander Witte picked up the top-secret folders and walked briskly out of the admiral's office. The man responsible for every navy SEAL on the planet stared out over the blue ocean. What's happened to me? He mused. Why am I so concerned about how I look, about my career? Twenty years ago I'd have been jealous of these men, sure. But twenty years ago I would've cheered the decision to send SEALs, any SEALs. Have I become a whining, sniveling, staff puke worried only about getting my second star?

The admiral shook his head, recovering his sense of focus. I still have to cover my ass. I still need something in my back pocket if these three men fail. He put his hands on his hips and looked beyond the beach toward the horizon. Somewhere out there was a bright green country where he'd learned combat survival the hard way. Vietnam had been his test of fire. Admiral Fitzpatrick said a silent prayer asking God to protect his three SEALs.

## Republic of Panama

Boone scratched his head. "I'll tell you what, boss, these maps don't help us for shit! I mean, take a look at the overhead photography. All the paths, rivers, or streams we might want to use for navigation, are invisible on the photos. They're all covered up by triple canopy jungle! I don't know how the hell we're going to find any legitimate landmarks."

Oby slid over to see what Boone was talking about. He studied the overhead photography and then checked the map. "Yep, sure as shit, this is going to be a ball buster! We won't know where we are and the movement through this crap will be nearly impossible. You know boss, if they put a time restriction on us we won't be able to adhere to it for certain. You know as well as I do that it takes about two hours to quietly patrol a thousand yards over broken ground. It takes about four hours to move the same distance through jungle like this during the daytime. But to move a thousand yards through the jungle at night will require at least eight hours!"

"So what do you suggest, tell them we can't do this?" Matt asked, stepping back from the dry erase board where he'd been scribbling comments and unanswered questions related to the mission.

"Now you know better than that, LT." Oby ignored Matt's jab. "I know Boone's the scout guy and all that, but the way I see it, this base camp is supposed to be on the river, correct?"

"Go on, you have my attention," said Matt.

The SEAL sniper continued. "Well what if we say the hell with all this jungle bullshit and go straight down the river? You know like navy guys. SEALs and shit!"

Boone moved to the map table again to take another look. The point man looked at the map for a second then locked eyes with Matt. "You know what, boss? Oby's right! If we can get inserted up river from this base camp, just stick to the river move down stream under cover of night, we'll eliminate a whole lot of problems. Make it easier to find the camp too!"

"Yeah LT!" Oby chimed in. "We could use a rubber boat! Hell, we could even swim or use a scuba re-breather like our LAR fives!"

Boone piled on even though the argument was obviously the way to do the job. "Hell, sir, they wouldn't even see us coming."

Matt stood there taking it all in. He loved watching the wheels turning. This is what being in the teams was all about. All SEALs cared about mission success. They were constantly studying, trying to improve their knowledge of the art of war. Whenever a SEAL platoon sat down to discuss a new mission tasking, each man in that platoon knew he had a vested interest in the success of the mission. Every SEAL therefore invested a lot of time, energy and emotion into pitching ideas and debating possible solutions. The best ideas eventually ended up in the rehearsal cycle. During the rehearsal cycle everyone had a chance to give real-time feedback as well as review videotapes of the rehearsals.

Most team guys were cut throat when it came to criticizing each other but they had to be. This was the best way to bring out solutions that worked. Matt knew he was lucky to have Oby and Boone.

"So how do we get a rubber boat in there?" Matt asked. "Parachute drop?"

"I don't know, boss," Boone answered, realizing Matt had just approved the idea. "Seems to me we could either steal one from a village nearby, if there are any nearby. Or we could have a larger boat drag or carry a rubber boat to within launch range and then release us."

Oby disagreed. "You know what? That just ain't going to work. Everybody up and down that river's going to be wearing farmer duds not uniforms. And they hate the Columbian army. If they see anybody coming down that river in a military boat like our rubber F-470s, the word will be out, sure as shit. By the time we get down river the guerillas will be sitting there eating popcorn, waiting for the light show to begin!"

"What about dropping a boat or dropping a canoe from the back end of a helicopter," Boone thought out loud.

Matt looked at his point man. "You know what Boone, I think you have an idea there. Let's figure out what the distance is related to the base camp based on our target information. We'll set up a navigation plan to place us a realistic distance from the target area. If we don't use one of our rubber boats we need to procure a craft, something the locals would not pay much attention to as it floats by in the night. We may or may not want to bring along the re-breathers just as a method of getting from the boats to the shoreline. How about using a dugout canoe?"

"That would work!" Oby blurted. "A dugout canoe would have the same profile at night as all the other local boats. But where do we get a dugout canoe?"

"I'll take care of that boss." Boone spoke up. "I'll make a few discreet phone calls. I'm sure there are people around here that can help us out on that end."

"Great!" said Matt. "Oby, why don't you get a hold of our air force friends and see what kind of aircraft we can use to deploy the canoe."

"You got it, boss!" replied Oby. Things were moving along smoothly, thought Matt. They didn't have much time left, but this was always the hardest part of the mission. Figuring out how they were going to get access to the target area without getting caught. Once on target, their standard operating procedures for reconnaissance and surveillance would kick in. He loved it when things came together. Matt turned back to the dry erase board and continued writing the mission timeline on the board.

# CHAPTER SIX

## San Clemente Island–California

The SEALs grumbled as they jumped off the large navy truck and onto the hard ground. "Hey chief!" one of the men yelled. "What the hell are we doing out here?" Chief Sampson stopped dead in his tracks and scowled at the questioner.

"What the hell do you care, Jones? Your job is to go where the big boss in Washington tells you to go! Now start tossing that gear out of the truck and move it into the Quonset hut. Let's go people, we're burning daylight!"

The SEAL chief turned walked to where Lieutenant Stone was standing. He didn't seem to notice the mumbling and moaning going on behind him. "Hey LT!" The chief called out. "When are going to sit down and work on this training schedule?"

Jared Stone looked over his shoulder. The chief moved like a jungle cat. He was an intimidating personality, even among SEALs. Jared felt very lucky to him in the platoon.

"Well chief, I was just going starting to work on that very thing. Ensign Barton here has quite a few ideas to share."

Chief Sampson's face contorted in a show of mock pain. "Mister Barton, I'd really appreciate it if you just sit on the sidelines for this one. No offense, sir, but this isn't exactly a practice mission. How about the LT and I work out the schedule and we'll brief you on it when we're done?"

The young ensign's face fell. "But, chief, I'm an officer! I'm supposed to be the one who calls the shots, not sit back and watch."

Chief Sampson didn't want to put the young officer down. He needed to guide him toward the day when he would command his own SEAL platoon. SEAL platoon commanders were expected to execute very difficult missions. In the same situation, other services sent majors and lieutenant colonels to accomplish such complex undertakings. The navy and more importantly, the national command authority, knew SEAL platoon commanders were up to the job.

The chief let up a bit. "Look, sir, we don't have much time. Let us brief you on the training plan and you critique our decisions. That way we have to explain our logic and maybe you can find areas where we can do better!"

Jared watched the ensign's expression change. "Sounds like a plan to me, Dan. We could use your help tracking the range setup and ammo staging. What to you think?"

"I think the chief here is smart as a cat. I'll take care of the logistics, Jared. Let me know when you are ready for your big critique!" The ensign's tone made it clear he was not very happy. He spun on his heel and left for the operations shack.

"He's a good man, chief. We need to start giving him a bigger piece of the pie."

"I know sir," Chief Sampson said, watching the departing officer. "At least he has a spine. Did you see his eyes? I thought for a second he was going to take a swing at me!"

Lieutenant Stone laughed. "Well I'm counting on you to make sure that doesn't happen! So where were we?"

"Sir, I've been thinking. We can pull off the recon mission, no sweat. I'm more concerned with conducting a sustained operation."

"Well it's like this, chief. We're supposed to be rehearsing for a reconnaissance and surveillance mission. But you and I know the possibility of that happening is slim to none. I suggest we focus instead, on the very good chance we'll be tasked with the rescue job."

"LT, I'm with you on this one. In my opinion, the rescue contains several critical training issues. We're talking about getting everybody in the platoon up to speed on open terrain contact drills and jungle movement, stuff we haven't touched since we were designated an urban platoon. Room entry, precision shooting skills, yeah we're hot shit. But not in the jungle, we both know that."

"I see what you mean, chief." Jared was running down a mental checklist of critical skills. "What if we put the training schedule together in phases representing the mission scenario?"

"So we'll see what phases need work and strip down to fix the weak spots?" The chief was already plotting the phases in his head.

"Exactly!" Jared responded. "We run the whole mission, soup to nuts. Then we isolate the steps of performance that require the most training emphasis."

"Okay sir, so let's get started!" The chief pulled out his navy issue notebook. "Phase one, we assume the recon team does a bang up job and finds the hostages. They succeed in pinpointing the site with a global positioning system. We receive the uplink and X marks the spot."

Lieutenant Stone knew his chief was on a roll. "That's right, chief. We start planning our mission based on an accurate target location. That way we can hit the camp fast. Our platoon comes in, sends out a scout team to confirm the status of the target and the opposition. We determine the exact location of the hostages, collaborating with the three-man team already watching the base. Then, we roll right over into a direct assault, take down the target, and rescue the hostages."

"Check LT! Then we can work on moving the hostages out of the immediate target area and extracting the team from the environment. You string that all together and you've got all the mission phases."

"And, therefore, the training and rehearsal sequence," Jared added. "Have we missed anything, chief?

"No, sir, I think that's enough to deal with for now."

"All right," Jared said nodding. "Let's go with your plan. Get your initial planning cell together, have the rest work on setting up the training areas and logistics. We don't have a lot of time so let's try to get things rolling early this afternoon and aim for completion sometime in the early evening. Then we'll spend late evening going over everything. If it looks good we'll hit the ground running tomorrow."

The chief was nodding in agreement. "Then, the results of the rehearsal tomorrow will determine the training schedule focus from that point on. Got it, Boss!" The chief was satisfied they had arrived at a sound approach. He slapped the SEAL officer on the shoulder. "This will be a piece of cake, sir. It's not like we've never done this before."

The lieutenant nodded. "Yeah, chief, I'm not too worried about the training side of this. I'm more worried about getting shot at."

The chief's smile faded a little. "Yeah, I know what you mean. But shit happens sir. You can't sit around and worry about it, does no good to worry. Well, sir, I'm heading out!" The senior enlisted man left Jared standing alone and headed for the Quonset hut.

## Bordentown, New Jersey

Alice smiled warmly. Her daughter had the giggles. She'd played that stupid Barney tape a hundred times but her little Jackie never failed to enjoy it anyway. Alice walked over to the kitchen counter and picked up the business card lying there. The Pentagon officer had been polite but firm. He gave Alice the card with instructions to call if anything strange happened, anything out of the ordinary. He'd been reluctant to elaborate about the army's cause for concern.

She knew her father was in trouble and that threats had been made against her family and that of her brother's family in California. After breakfast she'd call the nice young man and tell him about the sounds outside the house last night. Alice looked back again at her daughter. Time to start the day in earnest.

The bomb blast rocked the sleepy little neighborhood, the shock wave so intense it damaged homes over a hundred yards away. Car alarms wailed in every direction, reacting to the violent explosion. At ground zero, Alice's small three-bedroom house stood engulfed in flames. Throughout the neighborhood people sheepishly crept out of their homes to see what happened. There was nothing left of the once beautiful home.

"Oh my God, somebody do something!" yelled one of the neighbors as more and more people gathered to stare in shock at the devastating scene.

"I've called 911!" shouted another person nearby. "They are in the house! The family is still in the house!" Within minutes sirens screamed in the distance. The assembled neighbors realized that no one could have survived such a blast. The Sunday morning attack caught the entire family asleep in their home. "This is so terrible," one lady remarked. "So terrible. They had been through so much lately!"

"What do you mean?" a man asked.

"Didn't you know?" she said. "That poor woman's father was kidnapped not to long ago. He's an general stationed in Panama. So much tragedy in one family."

"Oh yeah, that's right." he remembered. "The general, the guy down in Columbia. Sure I remember the story now." The flames licked higher and higher. It was evident to anyone observing that the fire trucks would be too late.

## San Diego, California

Army Captain Chuck Alexander stared straight ahead. The road wound back and forth across the broad expanse of mountainous terrain. He didn't seem to notice, having traveled this way many times. He glanced at the digital clock imbedded in the dashboard, they were making good time. The young family was on its annual pilgrimage to a special little spot they knew, a garden untouched by development. As usual Chuck would set up camp tonight. Maybe if they had time they could even go hiking.

The long drive gave the officer time to think about his father. He knew the old man was a tough son of a bitch but Columbians didn't play by the queen's rules of war. There was a very good chance his dad wasn't going to make it out of this mess alive.

Chuck's thoughts were interrupted by a loud bang near the rear of the vehicle. A second later another explosion buckled the hood. Chuck immediately realized he couldn't steer the car. His last images were of his wife screaming and the faces of his frightened children as the car jumped the low concrete wall at seventy miles per hour.

It took an hour for the first rescue teams to arrive. They were specially trained to conduct difficult mountain rescue operations. A small crowd of police and firemen stood at the roadside containment wall, staring down at the now smoldering wreckage. It took an hour for the first member of the rescue team to return from the car sixty feet below.

The vehicle was too damaged to determine whether they'd been struck by another vehicle. One of the on-site investigating officers quickly wrote down the rescue worker's initial assessment. The tags had been traced to a Charles Alexander, an active duty army officer. Something seemed familiar about the name.

"You know what Phil? This guys last name sounds familiar," he said, turning to the other police officer.

"Hmm, Alexander…" the other policeman responded. "Let me see. Yeah, I've heard this guy's name before, too. Isn't there some army big-wig in the news with the same last name?" Both police officers shrugged their shoulders. They'd know soon enough. It would take a week or so before they connected the dots and confirmed the car had been taken out by two command detonated explosive devices.

## The Pentagon–Washington, DC

The intelligence officer stepped into the room and placed a blue folder on the chairman's desk. The nation's senior military officer nodded. "Thank you Johnson," he said without looking up. He waved his hand dismissing the junior officer. The chairman opened the folder and began speed reading the incident reports. They didn't add much to what he'd already learned watching CNN. The report was full of facts and witness accounts explaining the events of the previous days.

Domestic terrorist acts? For what purpose? Why kill two innocent families on either side of the country? He scanned the FBI white paper outlining their assessment. The FBI determined the deaths were part of a vendetta, a sophisticated pair of professional assassinations. Somebody had marked General Alexander's children for death. The FBI noted at the end of its white paper they were scouring the country for leads.

The final piece of the report was a CIA commentary on the possible motivations for the kidnapping in Columbia. The chairman's eyes were drawn to the fourth point on the list of probable causes. Why eliminate family members when they have the general in their hands. It didn't make sense. That is unless the FBI's viewpoint is correct. It is an old style Columbian vendetta. A righting of wrongs to recover lost honor. No, the hostages weren't taken for ransom, the need to satisfy a shortfall in guerilla financing. These actions were motivated by hate.

The chairman hit the intercom button. "Hey Sam," he barked.

"Yes, sir!" responded the aide.

"Could you come in here? I have a task for you." The general wanted to know more about the man indicated as the fourth probable cause in the CIA report. He wanted to have all his ducks in a row before speaking to the president.

"I'll be right there, sir, I'm on my way!"

The chairman released the intercom button and leaned back in his chair. He hated this office. The walls were covered with memorabilia from his long career. Awards, plaques, gifts, and of course lots and lots of pictures of the chairman when he was a warrior. The man in those photos looked back at him now. Slightly overweight, sitting behind a desk. The room had the air of a museum. It always gave him the feeling that he'd died and someone had set up a place where others could visit and learn something about the man who had been the Chairman of the Joint Chiefs of Staff. If he had his way he'd be in a desk right in the center of the operations and plans division of the Pentagon where all the hubbub and activity was occurring. Where brilliant young officers and enlisted men studied thick intelligence reports and embassy briefings trying to determine what the United States should do next.

The chairman put his hands behind his head and rocked gently back and forth. If this man, Chavez, is responsible, we need to find out quickly. If it wasn't him, we need to find out if there's a completely new personality working against them.

## Fort Sherman, Republic of Panama

The warehouse was empty of everything but six long folding tables erected for the benefit of the SEAL's recon team. It was quiet here. Matt had asked to be moved to the Atlantic side of Panama to be away from the interference of U.S. Military activity at Rodman Naval Air Station and Howard Air Force Base. Although a U.S. Military facility, Fort Sherman was a sleepy sort of place, focused primarily on conducting jungle warfare training for the U.S. Army. Boone, Matt, and Oby already had their equipment laid out on the tables, two tables per man. One containing their weapons, their load bearing vests, personal equipment such as hand held radios, escape and evasion kits, flares, camouflage face paint, water, and food.

The second table held each man's German LAR Five scuba system. The LAR Five was a small chest mounted oxygen re-breather. It was capable of keeping a SEAL alive underwater for up to three hours without emitting telltale bubbles. The table also held a life jacket, fins, facemask, and aviator gloves with the fingers cut off. A weight belt completed the list. A few feet away from the equipment staging area sat a sixteen-foot long dugout canoe. The canoe was a Panamanian variation of the local canoes that they would find moving up and down the Ariari River, in Columbia.

The canoe was carved out of a large tree trunk. The wood fibers had special properties. When placed in water the wood swelled up to create a leak proof boat. The canoe and had been discreetly procured by army supply personnel in Panama City. The vessel was just large enough to handle all the equipment the SEALs would be carrying and the thirty-five horse power outboard engine. The engine cover was dinged up and dirty. Purchased locally, it supported the profile of a poor fisherman. Rather than using a brand new motor, Matt was banking on the idea the locals on the river wouldn't pay attention to a sputtering old workhorse pushing a canoe down stream.

Oby had thoroughly checked the engine out, running it in a fifty-five gallon drum filled with water. Other than a little wear and tear and a dented prop it checked out good to go. The three SEALs stood by their tables. They checked each other's equipment. Acting as inspectors for their swim buddies. This process helped them find things that they themselves had missed. A little bit of tape there to cover up a shiny spot, some spray paint here, tighten up something that might rattle and cause noise. Each little adjustment gave the three men reassurance that their equipment was ready to do the job.

Once the gear inspection was completed, Matt called them over to where a chalkboard was standing. There were four folding chairs staged in front of the board where two of the men sat while a third ran down his part of the mission plan. At any time, any of them could object to a procedure or argue with an intelligence assumption. They were a team of warrior equals and each man knew the score.

Boone naturally was responsible for navigation down the river and movement in and around the target area. He was also responsible for creating a coordination grid to use as an overlay on the target area. The grid marked off using an alphanumeric system. Letters down the left side, numbers across the top. Cardinal references such as south and north were difficult to determine at a glance. One couldn't fight and run holding a compass to his face. It was even tougher to figure out where you were in the jungle. By using the grid, the three SEALs would be able to reference an object or an activity by calling out the grid reference just like the game, bingo. It was a very quick down and dirty way for people that were not in the same location to identify objects rapidly. The coordinating data had been passed on to the assets supporting them so that they could quickly and accurately pinpoint targets.

Oby was responsible for the reconnaissance and surveillance phase of the operation. He briefed Matt and Boone on how he wanted to conduct the initial recon when they found the target site. Oby went over every detail of how he was going to setup the first surveillance hide. He explained how the observation shifts would rotate every two hours. One man watch, one man guard, one man sleep. The last thing Oby covered was the surveillance logbook, something all qualified snipers were familiar with.

"Why the hell do we have to use the logbook?" growled Boone. "I don't care about sniper SOPs! Why can't we just write down what we see like we usually do?"

Matt could see the lack of sleep and intense planning effort was wearing them down. Time to step in. "We're using the sniper log because I told Oby to do so. It's the best format we have to capture everything and anything. Case closed!"

Matt's tone startled Boone. "Okay sir, you don't have to get your panties in a bunch!" Boone waved at Oby. "Go on brother SEAL, do continue!"

Oby smiled. "Happy to! A surveillance logbook is maintained by the surveillance team showing the time, place, activity and impact of every event as it occurs in the target area. While we SEALs may not think all the information is important, during the post mission debriefing intelligence professionals can pour over the log book and match its data with that of other reports they have on the target. It has to be neat and accurate. That's all, boss!" Oby sat down.

Matt was the last one to brief. He began by covering the command and control aspects of the mission then moved on to discuss how they were going to load the canoe into the helicopter. Matt detailed the radio frequencies, call signs, code words, and the use of fire support if and when they needed it.

"We have two primary and secondary extraction plans. One for us and one if we go out with the rescue force." Matt spent the next twenty minutes pouring over the details. In a way having only three SEALs made it much easier to plan. They didn't have to explain a lot of things to each other and they didn't have to invent SOPs. They'd worked together before and knew how each other thought and moved. There were no doubts about their individual skills as SEALs and no doubt of each man's courage under fire.

Matt looked at his watch, the planning effort was complete. "That was a great presentation. You guys have really done a great job on this. We have about thirty minutes before we rehearse the helicopter/canoe insertion. Grab something quick to eat and meet me out front."

"Okay boss." Oby said yawning.

"I'm moving now," Boone added. The two enlisted SEALs stood up and walked over to a table where some sandwiches had been prepared and left for them by the army cooks. Matt checked his watch one more time. Ten more until the mission started. Ten hours to go over the details in his mind a million times. Ten hours to wonder whether or not Senior Chief Auger was still alive.

# CHAPTER SEVEN

## *Ariari River, Columbia*

Auger watched the young men practicing their war fighting skills off in the distance. The makeshift firing range was only a few yards back from the riverbank. The far shore provided a simple impact area for the rounds as they zipped across the flowing water. The bullets made loud slapping sounds as they hit the mixture of clay and mud. All things considered, Auger couldn't help but critique their efforts. The guerillas were firing a mixed bag of weapons; one or two rifles, a few automatic weapons from various countries, and one or two submachine guns.

The small caliber SMGs, were virtually useless here in the jungle. Most submachine guns fired a nine-millimeter round, a bullet originally designed for use in pistols. The nine-millimeter had very little penetration power and while it could put out a lot of rounds, it failed to blast through the dense jungle where bullets were slowed down or deflected harmlessly. On the other hand the rifles employed by the fighters utilized the deadly and highly effective 7.62 NATO round, excellent for punching through just about anything. One drawback however, was the fact that most of these rifles used five-round magazines. Not nearly enough bullets per magazine to lay down a heavy base of fire during a fierce jungle contact.

Jungle warfare tactics were considerably different then tactics employed in other regions of the world because you rarely saw the face of your enemy until you were right on top of him. Ambushes set on jungle trails were established within two three yards of the intended course of enemy movement. The close proximity was critical so the ambushers could see at whom they were shooting. Once an ambush was initiated and the lead started flying the ambushers and their victims were locked nearly toe-to-toe in deadly combat. In this situation, having weapons that pumped out a lot of penetrating firepower was the difference between victory and defeat.

The rifles the men practiced with were better suited for wide-open spaces. In desert and mountain environments a man with a good rifle could kill you from half a mile away. The mixed bag of weapons made perfect sense to Auger. These guerillas were probably picking up weapons wherever they could find, buy, or steal them. He watched intently as one skinny fellow in charge shouted, expressing his displeasure at how a particular lad was reloading his SMG. The fact they were even spending time on reloading drills impressed Auger. That implied the man in charge had received some type of formal military training, maybe in the Columbian army or civil militia. Auger's experience told him most of the time untrained irregular troops just fired the rounds they had in the weapon and then high tailed it out of the line of fire.

As the American watched, a new group of men sauntered up to the makeshift range and took their positions on line. The first group fired their last shots and greeted the newcomers with laughter and animated gestures, telling their fellow warriors how well they'd done. The second group seemed organized a little better. Their equipment appeared to be more uniform also. Auger watched the supervisor of the first group, relinquish control of the range and walk away and another gentlemen, who had the demeanor of a man of some substance, took over.

"Can you see anything senior chief?" The general lay in the fetal position wedged into the cage in such a way his view was restricted to only the jungle.

"Just a bunch of camp goons wasting ammo down on the range!" the SEAL quipped. "They don't seem to be very proficient with weapons."

"How good do you have to be to shoot an American general locked in a bird cage?" he said. Auger grunted, acknowledging the wisdom of the older man's observation. These guys didn't have to be trained Special

Forces troops to put a world of hurt on their two American captives. The dynamic leader of the second group stepped forward and shouted a crisp command. The shooters immediately complied, assuming the proper firing posture and opening up, stitching the mud on the opposite side of the river in smooth three round bursts.

Every man was focused on attaining a tight impact zone, using the splattering mud to guide them. They soon began practicing reload drills, firing ten rounds then reloading until all six of their thirty round magazines were emptied. These guys were good, Auger thought. They were actually aiming the weapon and hitting what they wanted to hit. Their reloading was smooth as well. After ten minutes or so Auger realized the men on the riverbank weren't holding back on the ammo. Whoever they were they were the studs of the camp.

The supervisor, man in charge, or whoever he was, changed the drills and mentored those guerillas having problems. This unit had operated together and trained together for quite some time, Auger believed. They were also older than the first group using the range. Auger's mental image of the guerilla's capabilities shifted a bit. He now classified the inhabitants of the camp into two distinct elements. The hard-core rebels or guerrillas that seemed to have been doing this for quite some time were equipped much like their western counterparts. They had full combat vests with magazine pouches, canteens, knives, utility packs mounted either on their back or attached to the base of their vests, and medical supplies. Most were armed with AK forty-seven assault rifles and universally wore the same jungle pattern fatigues. Auger counted approximately twenty-five of these well-equipped, well-trained troops in the camp.

The vast majority of the camp's inhabitants, however, were the second type of combatant. They were much younger, somewhere in the range of nineteen to twenty years old. They were draped in a hodgepodge of equipment and carried a strange mix of weapons. From what the SEAL could observe, most of these men didn't use load-bearing equipment and no pouches or any other kind of survival equipment gear adorned their bodies. This indicated to Auger that this group likely didn't venture very far from camp. Many, of course, were raw recruits. The guerrillas he surmised, probably brought in a new crop of trainees each season, worked them, and then selected the best of the group to either to replace the causalities in their primary guerrilla force or to infuse the primary guerrilla force with new blood.

Senior Chief Auger had observed first hand the guerrillas ability to conduct ambushes in the jungle. They possessed good communication skills, were well lead, and well equipped. No doubt, Auger thought, due to all the cocaine money funneled to them by various drug lords. The symbiotic relationship between the guerrillas, who needed safe havens and a constant flow of manpower and material, and the drug lords who needed protection for their laboratories and their growing fields was well known.

"Well I'm sure the Army Rangers or SF will be here soon," said the general.

Auger twisted to look at the senior officer. "What makes you think they'll send the army in here? We're next to a river general. My guess is they'll send my buddies in here to save our asses!"

"Sailors? I seriously doubt it son. They'll never send sailors to do an infantryman's job. These assholes would chew up your frogmen!" The general's words were delivered with a bit more contempt than Auger could ignore.

"With all due respect sir, I've never met a marine or army puke who qualified to clean my rifle, let alone pull off a job like this one! I'll wager you a case of beer, American beer, that they do the smart thing and send the navy."

"I'll take that bet senior chief!" General Alexander's voice was getting weaker. Auger could see the beatings had taken a toll on the older man.

Loud shouting from down below interrupted the debate. Auger twisted his body back around in the small cage until he was able to see the rest of the camp through a small space between his knees. Down below his little perch the guerrillas had gathered around two white males. From their well-groomed hair cuts and fancy clothing Auger guessed they might be corporate types, probably from one of the cities.

Kidnapping executives of multinational corporations working and operating in Columbia was a lucrative sideline for the guerrillas. They would hold these gentlemen for two to three weeks while they negotiated a ransom. Eventually the hostages were freed with the insurance companies paying the freight.

As Auger watched the two men were ushered into a low one-room building that compared to his accommodations seemed like the Hilton. The door was slammed shut and locked. Strangely enough Auger was beginning to feel more comfortable. His inside reconnaissance of the guerrilla camp had his mind functioning again like a professional. There was a lot to learn that could be important later on down the road especially if he tried to escape, or more hopefully, if the good guys showed up. What a show that would be, he mused. Auger knew the Columbians would be no match for Delta Force or SEALs flying in with guns blazing, pinpointing the scrambling guerrillas with laser aiming systems, taking people efficiently with double taps to the head. It would be devastating and it would be quick. Hopefully, Auger thought, both he and the general would be alive when they arrived.

## SEAL Training Area–San Clemente Island, California

Lieutenant Stone knew instinctively they'd have to do it again. His platoon was trained and polished in the art of hostage rescue but these open field maneuvers, basic patrolling, and reconnaissance techniques were buried so deep in his men's memory banks they were fumbling around like rookies. That was one of the problems when a SEAL platoon focused on one specific mission area. You get good at what you practice and the rest falls to shit.

He turned to see a red-faced Chief Sampson wandering from platoon member to platoon member handing out his two cents worth on what he thought had gone right or wrong with the rehearsal. Very little from what the lieutenant could over hear had gone right, according to the chief. Sampson was an expert at dressing down the boys without breaking their spirit. The fact he'd spent a tour as a BUD/S instructor added a certain edge the men could appreciate. The men in this platoon trusted and respected the chief's judgment. His criticism stung only because the words rang true.

The lieutenant knew Chief Sampson didn't have to make anything up. They'd sucked, and sucked bad. The SEAL platoon had rehearsed the basic scenario of patrolling, approaching the objective, staging the rescue team on target and attacking. It wasn't working and the fact that the men were tired wasn't an excuse to stop and take a break. They would be far more fatigued when the action actually started as they moved through the jungle. Four or five of the men in the SEAL platoon had extensive experience doing cross training exercises in Malaysia and in the Philippines. Some had also participated in the training activities in Thailand.

The chief finished his walk about and released the platoon for a needed water break. He strolled back to where Lieutenant Stone stood, kicking up the dust with the tips of his boots. The chief was dragging ass a little. Stone waited for the chief to come within range and then asked the key question. "Well, chief, how bad is it?"

Chief Sampson kept his head down for a moment before looking up. "LT, I think this whole deal stinks."

"What do you mean?" asked the puzzled officer.

"Well, sir, it goes like this. We have some of our SEAL brothers out there putting eyes on target. When these guys are in place they can easily direct the rescue force."

"Yeah, so, I don't follow where you are going with this, chief." Stone was more concerned with the enlisted mans demeanor. Something was really bugging him.

"Well, LT," the chief continued. "We're a hostage rescue platoon. You know, as well as I do, what the downside is of focusing a SEAL platoon on a specific mission area. Now, sir, we're great at kicking down doors and taking precision shots at terrorists and such but we haven't spent shit for time practicing open field maneuvers and contact drills. Our guys are so rusty it's like we never even worked together!"

The lieutenant still didn't see where the chief was going with this little chat. "So what is your point, chief?" The LT's voice was firm, indicating he wanted the other man to finish his monologue.

Chief Sampson looked his officer in the eye. "My point is this boss, we shouldn't be doing this mission. As much as I like to go to these shoot and loot gigs, this platoon shouldn't be going into the jungle. I've no doubt that we could get the job done once we're inside the target area but there's a good chance we could get our ass handed to us patrolling through that mess. The locals know the terrain, are acclimated as well, they have the upper hand. I just don't have any confidence this platoon is going to react the way a SEAL team platoon is supposed to react, and that's my bottom line."

Stone put his hands on his hips and looked up into the blue sky. Whether he agreed with Chief Sampson or not, in a SEAL platoon the main player was the chief petty officer. A smart naval officer didn't make a move without the chief's understanding and agreement. The rest of the navy knew that too. It always had sayings like "the strength of the United States Navy is the chief petty officer", printed on coffee cups, plaques, and tee shirts. Lieutenant Stone knew it went double in the teams.

Stone realized that if he continued to push this platoon, took them into combat, and got men killed, not only would he be liable legally and morally, but also professionally. He'd be washed up in the teams if he was wrong. The word would get out that he'd been told by his chief he shouldn't do the mission, that the men weren't ready for it the challenge. The SEAL community would then assume that the glory-seeking officer overruled his chief's objections in the pursuit of kudos.

The platoon commander stared back looked back at his chief. "Chief, this is pretty serious stuff here. If you're asking me to pick up the phone and tell somebody we can't do this job, I need you to stand side by side with me, probably all the way up to the top."

The chief nodded, "I know it's damn serious sir. But what's even more serious is our responsibility to these men. I'm sure there's a platoon at SEAL Team Four fully capable of executing these mission parameters.

Their platoons are superbly trained and focused on jungle warfare. They have enough guys with rescue skills to put together an assault element. I mean, we are not talking about going into a five-star hotel here. The target consists of huts and lean-tos. On one side of this equation, we are over qualified on the other side we shouldn't be going in the way we look right now."

The lieutenant knew what he had to do. "Well let's go ahead and stand the men down for an hour. I'll make the call and wait for the shit to hit the fan. You and I should standby to fly back to the coast or at least participate in a conference call. Do we have the secure line hooked up?"

The chief was relieved. "Yes, sir, the secure line is hooked up and we have the ability to patch five lines in on a conference."

"Good deal, chief!" the lieutenant said starting to regain some of his confidence. "I think the logic is sound and we have had enough rehearsals to confirm what you are saying is true. I would put this platoon up against anybody when it came to breaking down doors and popping somebody in the forehead with two rounds but this is different. I'll go ahead and make the call, you do what you have to do, chief."

Sampson gave the officer a thumbs-up and marched away with his face set in grim determination. He was under no illusion his observation would be applauded by the higher ups. The LT might be a good troop leader but that meant nothing to the pukes who left the real work of the teams two or three promotions ago. Many of the officers in the staff in the senior command levels felt politics and saving face were more important than putting the right people in the target.

Lieutenant Stone walked to the Quonset hut where the secure phone was located. He spotted a few of his men sitting around and drinking causally. He tried to hide his concern about the mission but the SEALs could see by the look on his face that something was wrong. Most of the men believed the LT was upset about the botched rehearsal cycle. They would be very upset if they knew the truth, that their leader was about to request they abort the use of their platoon for a real world combat operation.

Jared Stone sat on the dusty chair and dialed the number to the operations officer of Special Warfare Group One. After three rings the phone
was answered. "Special Warfare Group One quarter deck, Petty Officer
Johnson speaking, May I help you, sir?"

"Petty Officer Johnson this is the platoon commander of X-Ray platoon. I need to talk to the operations officer if he is in."

"Sir, the operations officer went home for the day. Can I take a message?"

"That's a negative," Stone said quickly. "Call him at home, tell him I
ordered you to have him contact me. Make sure you convey it's a very
serious problem. If you can't get a hold of him at home call his beeper
and put in the beeper code for a phone recall. He has my number here
on the island, tell him he needs to call me on a secure STU line."

"Yes, sir!" the quarterdeck watch answered dutifully. "Will do!" The
quarterdeck watch hung up the phone. The lieutenant placed the handset back in its cradle and leaned back in the chair, sliding down a little
bit further to get more comfortable. This is really going to stink up the
place, Jared mused. The big boys are going to do everything from accusing us of being cowards to saying that we are trying to dodge a trip so we
can stay home with our families. The navy lieutenant knew for a fact
that the senior staff types wouldn't see the crystal clear logic of the
chief's complaint. Somehow, Stone pondered, he had to come up with a
strong enough argument to get his platoon off the hook for this mission.

## Naval Special Warfare Command–Coronado, California

The admiral walked into his spacious office, slamming the door
behind him. He'd received a cryptic phone call from the duty officer to
come into work to handle a secure STU call from San Clemente Island.
The top SEAL had traveled all the way from San Diego's Mission Valley
during peak rush hour traffic for the privilege of speaking to a lieutenant.

Admiral Fitzpatrick sat down behind his large walnut desk and punched the pre-dial button on his telephone. The automated system dutifully dialed up the Naval Special Warfare Group One operations officer, located a half a mile away on the Navy Amphibious Base, Coronado. The operations officer answered the phone after one ring. He handed the phone to the man in charge of the West Coast SEAL community, Commodore Robert Morris.

"What the hell's going on Bob?" said the admiral through clenched teeth.

"Well, sir, the commodore responded, the platoon commander of X-Ray platoon has requested that we relieve his platoon of their assignment." The commodore took a deep breath.

"What?" yelled Admiral Fitzpatrick, causing the commodore to jerk his head away from his own handset. "You dragged me in here because some lieutenant is getting cold feet? What the hell's going on here? Where did we get this guy?" The commodore took a deep breath and began to convey the platoon commander's logic.

"Admiral, I happen to believe he's right. Lieutenant Stone's concern and that of his platoon chief is that their specialized platoon is ill-suited for an engagement in the jungle. They are a highly trained HRT platoon. While they excel at hostage rescue team skills they're having great difficulty making up the deficit in jungle training in the time allotted them."

The admiral was having great difficulty controlling his temper. "Bob, they're SEALs damn it! I was against this specialization bullshit from the very start! What am I supposed to do now? Send an East Coast platoon from SEAL Team Four?"

The commodore suddenly realized the real problem. East Coast–West Coast politics. The old man was supposed to be in command of both. It was clear he was trying to throw a bone to his West Coast alma mater. "Admiral these men haven't touched an M-60 machine gun or conducted open field fire and movement in almost two years and they don't have much time left. They could receive the green light call to launch a rescue at any moment. Sir, the bottom line is simple. If they don't feel they're ready, my recommendation is we reassign the mission to the east..."

"Bob, I don't care what you think, and I don't care what that lieutenant thinks. This is a West Coast show. Nobody, and I mean nobody, is going to tell me who goes on a mission and who doesn't. I don't buy this crap about SEALs not knowing how to patrol and not knowing how to do fire and movement. If I remember right, this specialization shit was your idea!"

The commodore knew the admiral had him pinned to the mat. He'd been an advocate for creating super platoons capable of transcending all previous high water marks in every mission category. The old standard of SEAL platoons being "jacks of all trades and masters of none," was inhibiting the pursuit of operational excellence. In the new special operations era the national command authority wanted precision. Cadillac's not Chevy's.

The commodore tried one more time to convince the admiral to change his mind. "Admiral, this is a request from the platoon chief and platoon commander. If we force them to do this mission against their recommendations we run the risk of a disaster. One we could've prevented. It's my opinion that a SEAL Team Four jungle warfare platoon would be better suited for this operation. Consider for a moment that the target is not a sophisticated hostage scenario in a built up urban area. It's nothing more than a bunch of huts, lean-tos, and makeshift buildings. There's no need for a precision hostage rescue team." The commodore stopped talking.

The admiral remained silence for a moment. Then through clenched teeth he answered the commodore's plea. "Bob, you will order that lieutenant to continue preparations for mission execution. You will tell them it's his responsibility to get those men ready for combat. You tell him that and when you are done telling him I want you to schedule a meeting. Next Tuesday-just you and I. We have some serious issues to discuss regarding the readiness of your SEAL Teams. Do you understand me?"

The commodore realized he had lost. "Yes, admiral, I'll pass on your answer and your orders."

"That right, Bob, my orders. Not suggestions!" With that the admiral slammed the phone down.

# CHAPTER EIGHT

## *Staging Base–Fort Sherman, Panama*

Matt fiddled around with his equipment for what seemed like the fourth or fifth time in the last hour. He knew all his gear was finally good to go. Both Oby and Boone were putting the finishing touches on their equipment. In the few minutes left to them before mission launch, they mulled over every detail of the operation. All of them worked the phases through, running down mental checklists in an attempt to detect something amiss.

Matt spent a lot of time thinking about his father. It felt like a million years since he'd been burdened with the issue of his old man. His father's hero status as a holder of the Congressional Medal Of Honor had cast a shadow over Matt ever since he was a young boy. He'd gotten over it by the time the operation in Egypt came along. His combat experience not only removed his low self-esteem, but also brought him closer to his dead father. It sounded silly but Matt still felt the man's presence during times of stress. He knew the old guy was watching right now, rooting for Matt to kick some ass!

For the past two years Matt had been sitting on his butt at the basic training course in San Diego fooling himself into thinking he might have a chance for a normal life. His focus had shifted off a warrior mind state and had focused instead on trying to establish a relationship with Tina. He wasn't sure if he was going to stay in the teams for the long haul. Most enlisted men tended to stay in the full twenty years. Officers would eventually rise up the ranks, finding themselves in the staff environment.

Matt feared the day when he would have to tell operating SEALs what to do while not sharing the risks they were taking.

He hadn't promised Tina anything and she'd never demanded he make a formal commitment. It was an unspoken understanding between the two of them. But Matt was aware that barring any change in their relationship, they were probably heading to a place where commitment was waiting with all its baggage. Of course now things were changing. The last thing Matt thought would've happen had happened while occupying a shore duty billet, a real world mission tasking. He still didn't understand how he'd become involved.

His mind was a storm of confused thoughts and pictures. He knew he should be focusing on the mission details but he kept swinging back to Tina. What must she be going through right now? Matt didn't say much to her when he got up and left. She wasn't a team wife so she'd never been through the command briefings for SEAL spouses. At least then she'd understand the protocols. Even so, he'd lied to her.

Matt had been sharp enough to say communications on the island were screwed up so she shouldn't try to contact him. Of course in the four or five days that had elapsed since his arrival in Panama he hadn't been able to send any word to her. He also understood there was no way he'd break operational security to get a hold of Tina. It was unfair to her, but that was the way it was, teams and shit! Matt realized deep down in his heart that he had an important decision to make. After this mission he would have to decide whether or not he wanted to remain a SEAL warrior or seek a normal existence with Tina. There was no way he could do both.

For now his mind was clear. His job was to take Boone and Oby into Columbia and save Senior Chief Auger. Boone and Oby had the same determined look and the same desire to pull their friend out of the mess he was in. The intelligence types continued to express their pessimism, telling Matt there was a little chance the two American hostages would survive their ordeal. At a minimum, they believed the enlisted SEAL was already dead since he wasn't valuable enough to ransom.

Something in Matt told him that his friend and mentor was alive. He looked to his right and peered through the open hangar doors. He watched the CH-47 helicopter crew loading the versatile aircraft. The dugout canoe was sitting nearby, mounted on a standard boat trailer. Matt observed the army aircrew take the trailer and roll the boat straight up into the cargo bay. The canoe was too long to fit neatly so the tail ramp would have to stay down for the flight. The ass end of the dugout poked out of the helicopter a good three feet or so, an acceptable situation according to the aircrew commander.

The overall load of boat, trailer and SEALs, was no problem for the heavy lift CH-47. One of the crewmen walked toward the mouth of the hangar and caught Boone watching him. The two professionals exchanged greetings. Both had a job to do and a shared desire to see this particular mission go well.

Boone walked over to Matt, "All right boss, the crew chief says it's time to saddle up!"

"Okay, Boone," Matt turned to pass the word. "Oby, it's time to roll!" The three SEALs gathered up their op gear and headed for the helicopter. The engines were cranking up, whining loudly as if in protest. Boone threw his gear into the canoe. The equipment needed to be secured in a way that prevented loss if the boat capsized during insertion. There were no connections inside the dugout to attach equipment so Oby had drilled holes along the rim and placed hooks in each. This created both hanging devices and snap points for the equipment packs. Then Oby finished the job by running a piece of parachute chord around the entire circumference of the canoe. This give the three SEALs even more flexibility to stow things where they made the most sense.

Matt and Oby lugged the outboard engine over to the boat and pushed it into the bottom of the canoe, secured it to one of Oby's hooks and double-checked the rest of the load. Boone went over the flight path to the river and down the river to the drop point with the pilots. The run down was over quickly. It was time to go. Boone walked back to where Oby and Matt stood near the tail ramp.

Boone gave his friends the thumbs up. The rotors were up to full speed now, making it impossible to be heard. Matt slapped Oby on the back and the sniper climbed into the aircraft, squeezing in between the canoe and the side of the helicopter. Matt and Boone followed in turn. The three men moved forward and sat down in the nylon web seats prepared for them. Matt put on the headset offered to him and checked in with the pilots.

The pilots waited for the final time hack and passing of the code word clearing them to launch. Oby raised the sleeve of his shirt and glanced at his watch. Only one minute left to go before the time hack. He saw Boone staring at him in anticipation.

"Not yet!" Oby shouted, trying to be heard over the engines. He held up a finger and shouted. "One more minute!" Matt wasn't paying attention having already closed his eyes. He leaned back against the nylon webbing stretched out behind him and tried to relax. There was no sense in sweating the small shit, he thought. Soon the code word would be received and the game would begin. The helicopter would lift gently turning left and right to ensure the controls were working. Then the war bird would dip its nose and streak them away from the lush green of Panama and on to their target, Columbia. Time enough to be worried then he mused.

As if on cue, the SEALs felt the rough lurching movement as the helicopter separated itself from the tarmac. The CH-47 rose up twelve to fifteen feet and paused while the pilots checked their flight systems. Once the check was complete, the nose dipped forward and the CH-47 took off. The mission was at long last beginning.

## Bogata, Columbia

Chavez had only just arrived in Bogata, traveling by armed motorcade from a small military airfield outside the city to his personal residence downtown. The final phase of his plan was about to unfold. On his orders, two more of General Alexander's family had been brutally murdered the day before in the United States. Now the stage was set for the final moment of vengeance. This last act had to be completed face to face, his family honor demanded no less.

Chavez made arrangements in advance to be escorted to the base camp on the Ariari River where the Americans were being held. Once in the camp he would have the pleasure of killing the man who had directed and ordered the death of his only son.

Chavez had many informants within the U.S. intelligence agencies telling him the Americans were convinced the general was being held somewhere inside the city of Bogotá. They had also informed him the U.S government believed the other American soldier taken hostage with the general, was dead. Chavez didn't care about the extra soldier. He would give him to the guerrillas to use as they saw fit. It was their decision to make, but General Alexander was not to be harmed.

The Columbian military had been paid handsomely to turn the other way. They pretended to search various areas, reporting their lack of success directly to the U.S. Ambassador. Nobody in the Columbian military was trying too hard to come up with that information. A little money in the right places, a few threats here and there, and the Columbian military was firmly in Chavez's back pocket. Most of the military leaders who would have opposed him, paused when they remembered how swiftly he'd dealt with the Columbian pilots who participated in killing his son. The Columbian military wanted to end the violence in their country but they were afraid to face the terror of Chavez's organization.

The phone rang. Chavez picked up the phone and listened for a moment. He slowly placed the receiver back on its cradle. Moving to his luggage, he pulled out the camouflage fatigues that he knew would help him blend in with his escort. It'd been many years since he'd personally patrolled through the jungles of his homeland. It might be a tough haul for him but he was determined to show the men of his escort that he was still a warrior.

## Howard Air Force Base, Panama

The C-9 transporting the X-Ray platoon touched down at Howard Air Force base and taxied toward a secure off load area. Large square cargo trucks referred to in the military as bread trucks pulled up along side. The side cargo door opened slowly and a bright yellow forklift promptly moved into position under the fuselage to receive and remove the platoon's equipment pallets. The airport support personnel scrambled to pack the SEAL's equipment into two six by six trucks staged on the apron.

Once the cargo was secured, the SEAL platoon exited from the rear of the plane. They went immediately from the bottom of ladder into a bus standing by with blacked out windows. Once the entire platoon was seated the small convoy of vehicles left the airstrip and headed toward an isolated hangar located near the beachside boundary of the base. The hangar was the designated isolation area for X-Ray's final mission planning phase.

Jared Stone waited patiently until the vehicle pulled into the hangar and the large metal doors were slammed shut. The heat was stifling. A navy commander approached Lieutenant Stone carrying a large yellow package. The SEAL officer stepped forward to greet the messenger bringing the final coordination data. The senior officer smiled and extended his hand.

"Here you go, lieutenant. You now have all the frequencies and communications information needed to conduct your operation. The reconnaissance mission has already been launched. We expect to begin receiving a real time feed of target data in seven or eight hours. For now, you're to focus on planning your infiltration. The helicopter crews are at your disposal. Ask for any other information that you need from us to complete your task. Use any information that the reconnaissance team provides you to modify how you might strike the target. You don't have a lot of time. I suggest that your men get as much rest as they can."

Jared nodded quietly taking the package, "Yes sir, thank you." Chief Sampson walked up as the staff officer departed.

"Problems sir?" he asked.

The lieutenant watched the staff officer leave the hangar. "What's that chief?"

"Never mind, lieutenant. So what's the good news?"

Stone was still immersed in his own thoughts. "Get a load of this heat, chief. I think you and I have to touch base with the aircrew. Have the rest of the guys chill out for a while."

"Sounds good to me, LT!" said the chief. "I'll have the rest of the platoon spread out in the hangar and stage their mission gear for a quick departure, then stand them down for a few hours. When do you want to visit the pilots?"

"As soon as you put the word out, chief. I'll wait here for you." The chief spun around and made his way to the gang of men nervously standing by the pile of equipment. Jared made a mental note to set aside enough time for a last personnel inspection with full mission gear. Jared wiped his brow with the back of his sleeve. Some of the men were already starting to look a little pink, he observed. The heat here was different than the desert. It was wet and sticky and seemed to zap your strength.

Chief Sampson passed the word for everybody to drink as much water as they could possibly hold. He knew from painful experience that dehydration snuck up on you when your body was preparing for battle. The heat just made it worse. He decided to have everyone add an extra canteen to the load out. They were already carrying about twenty-five pounds of water each. One thing was true about water, once you consumed the precious liquid, you didn't have to carry it on your back anymore.

Lieutenant Stone walked over to a situation map pinned to a large bulletin board on the side of the hangar wall. The situation map showed the Ariari river area and the suspected location of the base camp where the two hostages were presumably being held. On a table nearby lay a metallic clipboard with the words Top Secret, printed in large red letters. Jared flipped the container open to reveal three inches of intelligence message traffic relating to the mission.

As he read through the first couple of messages he paused, a paragraph jumped out and grabbed his attention. A highly reliable intelligence source indicated that Chavez himself was going into the interior. Why would Chavez expose himself so recklessly? Moving further through the pile of detailed information, Jared discovered a CIA biographical assessment on Chavez and his operation in Columbia. The lieutenant had already been passed this information back in the United States, and was well aware of Chavez's violent background and his international financial dealings. But what he didn't realize, as he read this report, was that Chavez had lost a son, a son who died at the hands of the Columbian military while conducting his father's illegal operations in Columbia.

He'd been killed by Columbian air and ground troops, but the report went on to say that the counter narcotics sweep had been managed and directed by U.S. Southern Command intelligence assets, and General Alexander personally supervised the operation. While Matt hadn't seen any indication in any of the intelligence reports, it seemed clear to him that Chavez had the American general snatched as payback for the death of his son.

At the very bottom of the clipboard, Jared found a series of short messages indicating several members of General Alexander's family had been brutally murdered throughout the United States during the last forty-eight hours. Chavez was on a collision course with the United States and more specifically, X-Ray platoon.

Stone glanced around the hangar to see if any of the intelligence officers on the joint command staff were still standing by to assist the SEAL platoon. The platoon was alone in the large space. Maybe if he called for help somebody could come down and listen to his theory. Jared looked up at the clock on the wall and immediately dismissed the idea. There wasn't enough time to chase theories. He had real things to worry about now. X-Ray was scheduled to launch in two hours.

## River infiltration point, Ariari River, Columbia

The helicopter slowly dropped from its cruising altitude of fifteen thousand feet and settled into a low terrain contouring flight path, cruising a mere one thousand feet above the dark jungle below. The area around the river was mountainous. The helicopter pilots believed it should be possible to slide in under the Columbian radar by following the river basin. The Americans were attempting to conduct the operation without alerting the unreliable Columbian military.

The CH-47 helicopter was equipped with devices that muffled and muted the sound of its engines. The pilots were also flying with night vision goggles. There were no safety lights or navigation lights of any kind operating during the mission flight. Being seen or heard by people on the ground and having that alarm spread down the river was a very real concern.

Intelligence experts had explained that if the helicopter dropped in low enough the jungle below would dampen the sound of the rotors. Accordingly, the CH-47 dropped had down ten miles up river of the guerrilla base camp. After flying five more miles the helicopter dropped down another five hundred feet. The crew chief came back and gave Matt and his men their five-minute warning.

Matt woke up Boone by jabbing an elbow into the point man's ribs. Boone had fallen asleep while acting cool, pretending to be disinterested. Oby, Boone, and Matt checked the critical equipment connections one more time to ensure everything was in its proper place. The crew chief stood by his station near the nose of the canoe, ready to pull the quick release on the green light. The quick release held the canoe and its load under tension, retaining control while in flight. Once the green light flashed, the crew chief would disconnect the boat from the helicopter. The CH-47 would fly with a slightly nose up attitude to help the boat roll out of the aircraft.

The helicopter dropped another one hundred feet, so close to the river and the surrounding jungle Matt didn't want to watch. Even in the dark he could see the jungle canopy flashing by and the ominous mountains looming up on either side of the river.

I hope these pilots are good, he thought. If they screw this up we won't know what hit us. The crew chief listened to his headset, then turned holding up two fingers. Matt repeated the signal for the two-minute warning to Oby and Boone. The three SEALs positioned themselves on the left side of the canoe. Matt checked his watch one more time to confirm they were on schedule. They'd have two hours to move down the river and get near the base camp, and another thirty minutes to move inland to setup an observation position directly across the river from the base camp.

The crew chief moved a step forward to get Matt's attention. He held up one finger. This is it, Matt thought, again passing the one-minute warning signal to Boone and Oby. The three SEALs stood tall watching as the green light next to the tail ramp flashed on. The aircraft tilted up and the canoe was released. As rehearsed, the weight of the canoe forced it to roll cleanly off the boat trailer. Matt, Oby, and Boone began moving, trying to keep pace with the speed of the canoe's departure. They didn't want to fall too far behind and become separated from their boat in the dark. All three of them remembered to crouch down as they were exiting the aircraft.

Matt wasn't ready for the shock of the warm water hitting his body. It felt like bath water, he thought struggling back to the surface. He could see the bobbing heads of his two partners and moved with several power strokes towards the silhouette of the canoe.

The canoe stayed right side up, the dim red chemical lights marking its position. Matt had requested the pilot conduct the drop no higher than four or five feet above the water. A high drop would cause the canoe to tumble, possibly destroying some of the equipment inside or even sinking it. With powerful strokes Matt, Oby, and Boone reached the canoe. Matt and Boone stabilized one side of the canoe as Oby crawled inside. He quickly checked the equipment and gave Matt a thumbs-up.

Matt realized they couldn't hear the helicopter leaving the area. I guess that part worked the way it was supposed to, he thought. Boone jumped into the canoe next then Boone and Oby helped Matt scramble into his position in the middle of the boat.

Boone and Oby spent the next two or three minutes untying the outboard engine and getting it into position at the aft end of the boat. The dugout was flat providing a transom for the outboard motor. The motor was lowered onto this section of the boat and screwed into place. The lower part of the engine was then placed into the river. Oby messed around with the engine cover for a minute or so while Matt checked his watch. They were right on schedule. Boone and Matt both had their weapons out and were scanning both sides of the shoreline. Although the engine wasn't running, yet, the canoe seemed to be staying in midstream, pushed rapidly toward their objective by the current.

# CHAPTER NINE

The rough coughing sound of the outboard engine coming to life startled Matt. For the ruse to be effective the three SEALs must look like locals moving down the river on their way to a buddy's house downstream. Matt lowered his rifle and placed it across his lap. The three men weren't wearing any military headgear. To anyone watching along the shoreline they were just three guys in a boat.

Matt was beginning to get a bit concerned; they'd done too good a job making the engine sound like an old piece of crap. The outboard didn't sound like it was going to make it much further than the next bend. Boone reached inside the equipment pack stowed near his legs in the bow of the boat and pulled out a small transmitter. The communications device was just like the beacons carried by U.S. pilots for search and rescue response. He pushed a rubber-coated button and the beacon began emitting a pre-designated signal, specially coded to indicate the SEALs were safely enroute to the target.

The beacon was a great way to communicate the situation on the ground without spending too much time exchanging verbal signals. They didn't need confirmation the signal had been heard. It was only sent to make the boys back at headquarters feel warm and fuzzy about the progress of the reconnaissance mission.

Boone reached down in the pack again and pulled out a night vision scope tightly wrapped to avoid moisture. He patiently scanned both sides of the river looking for any hostile activity that might indicate troops set up on the river. Boone knew there was a fifty-fifty chance their mission had been compromised. If it was, the easiest way to take the SEALs out was to hit them with a river ambush.

The recon team flew down the Ariari River at a fairly quick clip using the steady current to help them. Matt didn't want to arouse suspicion by zooming down the river to get ahead of schedule. The average Joe out here was a poor fisherman or somebody going for supplies and returning back to his home. A real local wouldn't push their precious engines trying to get back home. In this part of the world things moved slow anyway.

The three navy men rode in silence for the next forty-five minutes. It was virtually impossible to determine how fast they were moving down the river and therefore difficult to figure out how much distance they'd covered. The boat was moving on a river whose current was moving at a good clip. Boone was first to notice the problem. He poked Matt, jabbing him in the shoulder to gain his attention. Boone pointed to the bottom of the boat. "Aqua!" he said, with a poor Spanish accent. "Mucho aqua!" he continued sounding alarmed.

Matt looked but wasn't able to see anything, so he reached down with his hand and felt around. His fingers plunged into six inches of river water lying in the bottom of the canoe. The scooped out interior of the canoe was shallow. The design allowed enough room for a few people sitting one behind the other, leaving the sides 3-4 inches thick, hence the weight.

The particular type of wood the locals used when building the canoes was porous. It was expected to swell once placed in the water. The swollen wood acted as an effective water proofing technique making the boats virtually unsinkable. So Matt didn't understand how water could possibly have seeped into the boat. He leaned forward and whispered to Boone. "Ya think this is from the drop?"

Boone considered it for a moment then shook his head. "No way, boss. When I was scrambling around looking for the radio it was bone dry down there. The water's been rising steadily for thirty minutes!" Matt reached outside the edge of the canoe to feel how much free board there was between the top of the canoe and the river's surface. The canoe was noticeably lower. There was no accurate way for him to determine how fast the water was coming in or whether it was still coming in.

Oby couldn't hear what the other two were whispering about so he reached out and kicked Matt in the leg. Matt scooted backwards to get closer to his sniper.

"What the hell's going on?"

"The canoe has water in it," Matt said. "Hey look out!" Oby had inadvertently steered to the right when Matt started speaking. "Make sure you keep this thing in the middle of the river Oby." Oby shoved the tiller hard over to the right moving the canoe away from the dark line of jungle foliage at the edge of the river. He moved back into the river and resumed course. Then he leaned forward.

"So what, sir, it's probably from the insertion."

"It is not from the drop," Matt said. "Boone said it was bone dry when he went for the radio and it's getting worse as we speak!" In the short time the two SEALs had been discussing the leak, the water had risen another two inches. The depth of the inside of the canoe was only about eighteen or nineteen inches. If the wet stuff kept coming in at this rate they'd be sitting in a bathtub within in twenty minutes.

"Boys, I think we're sinking!" Boone expressed his alarm louder than a whisper but it went unnoticed by the other two men.

Oby was first to pose a theory. "You know, these boats are supposed to be water proof. They're carved from one tree trunk then put in the water so the wood can swell up. I mean they are virtually unsinkable."

Matt countered, "Yeah, yeah, yeah. I know all that but we still have water coming in."

Oby continued to explain, "Boss, we had this canoe out of the water for a good two or three days. It's possible this thing just dried out. I mean, consider how many cuts and cracks this boat had. It's likely the water rushed right through since the wood shrank in the heat. You know, I didn't think to check the bottom of boat even once it was staged on the trailer."

Matt moaned, "Shit Oby, I see what you mean!" Meanwhile Boone was getting tired of trying to decipher the quiet debate going on in the back of the boat.

"What the hell are you guys talking about?" said Boone. Matt leaned forward to bring his frustrated point man up to speed.

"Oby thinks we left the boat out on the trailer too long and it dried out. The holes and dings in the bottom of the boat would have gotten bigger once the wood shrunk in the sun."

Boone nodded in the dark. "Makes sense, so we are a bunch of dumb shits! Now what? Do you think this thing's going to swell back up in time?" Matt checked the depth of the water again—it was now ten inches high.

"I don't think so," Matt said to Boone. "It looks to me like we are going to be swimming and we are going to be swimming fairly soon." Oby had a suggestion.

"Sir, why don't we try to increase the speed of the boat and get as much distance as we can before it sinks completely." Matt agreed. They were still a good eight miles out from the target, every mile reducing the chance they'd have to abort the mission. Matt decided to push on.

The three men traveled in silence. Matt had a million things flying through his mind. Using the LAR Five scuba was out of the question now. They would have to leave them secured in the boat and hope to come back after Operation Green Dagger was over. Could they swim all the equipment the objective or should they go on land and hump through the jungle? In BUD/S training, every SEAL candidate had to swim five nautical miles. Five nautical miles was equivalent to seven land miles. If they could get another mile or so out of the boat they'd be within swimming distance. It would be the same as BUD/S, except for the fact people might start shooting at them as they floated down the river.

Boone must have been thinking along the same lines. He moved closer to the SEAL officer and whispered in his ear, "Well boss, at least we don't have to worry about navigation, just point our nose down stream and start stroking!"

Matt agreed, "Yeah, and the river current will make the trip much shorter time wise. What do you think, should we keep all the equipment?"

Boone studied the question for a moment before answering. "Sir, I think we should keep everything with us. It's all waterproof and neutrally buoyant. All we should have to do is tow it along behind us or lay on top of it and float. We may need all that stuff before this job's over."

Matt made the decision. "Okay Boone, we'll take all the equipment."

By now the water had risen up to their waists. Luckily it was warm, SEALs hated cold water. "Let's untie the equipment while we can still find the equipment." Each of them found their personal gear and disconnected it from the boat. Then they snapped the equipment into their battle harness.

The SEALs were following the ageless standard operating procedure of keeping their vests and battle harness open at the waist and chest. Frogman learned long ago that it's impossible to get all the stuff off of you if you started to sink under the weight. This was standard procedure during peacetime training and in war. The neutrally buoyant gear should prevent them from plunging to the bottom of the Ariari River, but an SOP was an SOP. Once the equipment was snapped in, Matt indicated to Oby to drive the boat over to the right side of the river.

Oby noisily maneuvered the boat in towards the shoreline, all three of them getting smacked by low hanging branches they couldn't see in the dark. Getting out of the boat was a trick. Muddy bottom, swirling current, and trying to stop the boat long enough to jump out. Oby unscrewed the outboard motor from the transom, disconnected it from the fuel bladder, and dumped it over the back into the river. It sank immediately. Then he grabbed the fuel can and dropped that into the river, opening the can so the water would rush in and sink it faster. He was the last one to get out of the boat. The three SEALs assembled on the port side of the canoe.

When Matt saw Oby enter the water he gave his instructions. "All right guys, we stay in physical contact. We don't have buddy lines so if we get separated out here in the dark we'll never get back together again.

We're going to float down the river hugging the right hand side. We still have the fins in our equipment bags so I suggest we put them on but don't stroke hard, let the current do most of the work. Oby you go ahead and put your fins on first, then Boone, and then I will do it. Help the guy next to you."

Oby unsnapped the fins from the side of his equipment pack and put them on one at a time while Boone held on to his equipment harness. Once his fins were donned, Oby smacked Boone on the shoulder, holding him while Boone went through the drill. Matt was the last to put his fins on while Boone made sure he didn't float away from the group. The canoe was almost completely under water by now and painfully banging up against their knees.

Matt whispered to Boone, "Lets go!" The three SEALs separated from the boat. The water was so warm it actually felt good for the three of them to swim free and clear of that boat. Matt's butt had been getting sore from sitting on the hard wood anyway. His best guess was they had between six and seven miles of river to navigate and swim before arriving near the suspected location of the guerrilla base camp. The three men continued to stroke in silence. First trailing their equipment, but eventually placing it underneath their arms and kicking while laying on their bellies. Because of the current this seemed to be the most comfortable way to move down stream. This posture also allowed the men to keep their weapons at the ready in front of them.

They hadn't forgotten there were bad guys out there who wouldn't appreciate their little midnight swim. The hours passed uneventfully. Matt was the first one to recognize that they were getting dehydrated when his calf cramped up so bad that he couldn't move his right leg. He whispered to Oby and Boone to start drinking water. He followed his own advice, reaching down for his plastic canteen. Dumb mistake, Matt thought.

All SEALs knew that once you got inside the water, cold or warm, your body heat began to escape rapidly. Your body compensated by trying to change its fluid distribution to either cool down the body, or warm it up. For the last hour or so the three SEALs have been dumping body heat into the river.

Matt didn't felt chilled yet but the river no longer felt like bath water to him. The men were also burning a tremendous amount of calories. The current was helpful but the three SEALs were still pushing too hard. They couldn't forget the fact that one of their friends was waiting down river. Matt estimated they'd covered at least two miles, maybe three. If that was the case they had about another hour of swimming to go before they would have moved to the shoreline and determine their position using the GPS or global positioning system. Matt checked his watch, it was fifteen minutes after midnight. Another hour would put them around one o'clock. He figured the GPS check would probably take thirty to forty minutes if they did it right and set security.

That meant they couldn't be back in the river again until about two o'clock. Depending on how far away they were from the target area they would have to swim fairly quickly to get down to the target and get into their observation position, all before the sun came up.

After a long pull on his canteen, Matt returned to the task of swimming. Immediately he could feel a cramp in his left leg starting up so he relaxed. In a few minutes the cramp went away and he was able to start kicking again. For the next twenty minutes all three SEALs began to cramp up and alternatively assist each other through the pain until the water they consumed began to take effect.

This was slowing down their progress, Matt realized, but the current was still moving them in the right direction. Their initial intent to avoid people along the shoreline by detecting campfires with the right vision equipment had been discarded. The three SEALs had to hope that it was too dark to notice three blobs floating by. They were all conscious of this fact and maintained silence, whispering only when necessary. Matt glanced at his watch yet again, another thirty minutes and they would pull into the shore, just thirty more minutes.

## Guerrilla Base Camp–The Ariari River

Auger heard a commotion down the hill and to his left. There was apparently something important going on in the camp below. He didn't feel threatened. He'd been in his cage for some time now and his captors had kept their distance. Twisting his head to look down through his cage, Auger watched as two gentlemen that he didn't recognize, joined the guerillas. The strangers were talking excitedly to the other guerrillas around them. The senior chief could barely follow the conversation, then he heard the name Chavez.

Senior Chief Auger wasn't an intel-type but he wasn't an idiot either. He knew who Chavez was by deed and reputation. Anybody working in the southern command area of operations knew about the notorious Columbian drug lord. It appeared from the chattering below that Chavez was going to pay the camp a visit, and soon. A contingent of ten guerrillas moved off and began to prepare their equipment. He could see they were filling their canteens with water and stuffing food in their pockets. His best guess was this was the welcoming committee from the camp. Soon the ten men would move down the trail to link up with Chavez and his entourage.

The senior chief could hear the general sleeping nearby in his cage. The old guy hadn't said much. General Alexander wasn't whining or complaining, but it worried Auger that the guy was sleeping so much. Auger was glad he didn't have to baby-sit and worry about himself at the same time. Fifteen minutes later the ten-man patrol formed up and moved out of the camp. According to the navy man's calculations their departure reduced the number of shooters in the camp to about twenty. If the Americans were going to attempt a rescue, this would be the time.

Even worse, if they waited too long, the camp's firepower would be increased by whoever was coming with Chavez. Auger believed in his heart that somewhere out there, there were snake eaters planning a rescue mission. He looked around the edge of the jungle and then across the river to the other side. That's where I would be right now if I was watching this camp, he said under his breath. You can see the whole horseshoe shape of the encampment. A sniper could reach in and touch somebody without difficulty and you could sneak an assault force across the river to a final launch point right where the jungle touches the river. It'd be a piece of cake, he thought. Come in, hose everybody down who isn't an American, and let God sort them out. That is unless the general was correct and they sent in Rangers. Then the rescue would become a fifty-fifty toss up. A real Wild West show!

A black cloud seeped in on Auger's positive thoughts. A feeling that he was wrong. The little voice in the back of his mind had been growing in power. Its message was always the same. Nobody knew where he was and nobody was ever going to come to save him.

# CHAPTER TEN

## *Jungle Trail–Columbia*

Chavez tripped for what seemed like the hundredth time on an unseen root reaching out across the path. He was getting too old for this shit. The young men who were escorting him were taking it all in stride, this was their way of life. Chavez had grown soft in the last couple of years, flying wherever he wanted to go, limousine taking him here and there. His workout routine was strict but he never pushed himself that hard, not this hard.

They'd been moving on the jungle trail for three or four hours taking only one fifteen minute break. Chavez ran out of water quickly but the men around him realized that he was "el jeffe", the boss. All he had to do was look thirsty and he was offered a canteen. He was surrounded by approximately twenty-five of the warriors, warriors that he'd paid for and nurtured.

They were proud to be picked as his escort. Their plan was to link up with a group coming out from the base camp. They would link up near a large loop in the river where the trail meandered to within fifty yards of the fast moving water. The loop was easily visible from the air and a easy to identify when you were walking on the trail. Except for that terrain feature, the trail tended to follow a straight line moving north, by northeast.

Chavez peeked at his watch. He had about five hours of walking left to endure until link up at the rendezvous point. He knew he had to suck it up and put a good face on it. He must show these men that he was tough, tough like them. Chavez straightened his back and tried to walk with a sense of purpose. Nobody seemed to pay attention. They were too absorbed in patrolling and professionally scanning the jungle for threats. Five more hours, he thought, five more hours.

## The Ariari River–Columbia

It was time. Matt reached across to squeeze Boone's shoulder. Boone nodded acknowledgement and repeated the gesture, giving Oby the signal to swing in toward the shore. They only had twenty yards or so to swim until their feet touched the shallows. Boone, Oby and Matt formed a triangle focusing their attention on the potentially hostile riverbank. The three SEALs spent five minutes at the water's edge, looking and listening. Trying to absorb the natural sounds and condition of the jungle.

Boone was the first to crawl ashore. Oby slid alongside, covering the right flank of their small landing site. Matt pushed in between them to assume the point of a new defensive triangle. There wasn't a need for plans and commands the men instinctively knew what was needed. Oby was carrying the global positioning system or GPS, in a waterproof pouch. He now pulled the device from its protective bag and set up the system. Matt adjusted his body to pick up one hundred and eighty degrees of coverage so Oby could work.

They'd been in the water for a long time and the wind blowing down the river wasn't helping. To make matters worse, the three men had nearly consumed all their water. The muscle cramping had been a real problem, a problem they hadn't anticipated. Of course they hadn't planned on swimming all the way to the target either. It took Oby five minutes to orient the GPS and ensure that all the coordinates were set. He studied the digital read out and checked it one more time. The GPS was sophisticated enough that Oby could ask a question such as "what is the bearing and distance to my destination".

According to the GPS the bearing was parallel with the river but the distance was two hundred meters. Oby was stunned. He checked his figures one more time. It was hard to believe they could already be within two hundred meters of the base camp location. Maybe the intelligence guys plotted the camp's location incorrectly on the terrain map, thought the sniper.

Matt knew it was taking a lot longer than normal for Oby to get a GPS fix. He began to worry that maybe the GPS was suffering from a power failure. Good old map and compass skills were great, but here in the deep jungle the GPS was about the only thing that worked. Just then Oby closed the GPS cover and inched over to where Matt was lying.

"Hey LT!" Oby said. "The GPS says we're only two hundred meters up river from the base camp! I've checked it twice so there's no mistake."

Matt needed more confirmation. "Boone, pull out the M-911 night scope and scan south of here. Oby, take up security while I break out my map." Matt unfolded the waterproofed map. He needed to retrace their movement from the drop point to their present position. There had been two quick turns, first left, then right, just before the SEALs went feet dry. Each leg of the turn was about thirty or forty meters. Hopefully Matt could locate the feature on the map.

It was so dark Matt risked using his red lens flashlight. He shielded the light with his body to avoid interfering with Boone's efforts to use the M-911. Cupping the tip of the light with his gloved hand Matt followed the river, working his way back to the suspected location of the camp. He moved his finger back upstream from the camp and found what he was looking for.

There was the switchback turn in the river! He judged the length of each leg to be about forty meters. Matt knew this wasn't an exact science but if they were only two hundred meters away from the bad guys they were in position to start a reconnaissance in short order. Matt checked his watch. It was three thirty in the morning. If they moved through the jungle tactically it would take approximately an hour to get through that two hundred yards.

Another problem was visibility. They might have to go right up to the edge of the camp perimeter before seeing anything of value. That's why Matt had originally picked an observation point across the river with an unobstructed field of view. Matt pulled Boone closer to find out what the point man could see through the trees.

"Any luck, Boone?"

"Nope!" said Boone. "Nothing but black."

Matt wanted Boone's advice. Boone was a great point man and he'd have an opinion on their ability to move through the dense cover and make the timeline. "Boone, can we make it through this mess in the time we have left?"

Boone thought for a second. "No I doubt it. But I've got an idea boss. Why don't we go back into the river, move down about another hundred yards or so? That should only take about ten minutes. Then we'd only have to patrol one hundred meters through the jungle. By that time the M-911 should pickup campfires and lights in the base camp. If we do see that activity we will know we are right on target. We can move up to the edge of the jungle and determine whether or not we can establish an observation position. It is your call LT!"

Of course it was his call, Matt understood. It was always his call, his decision to make. What were the odds this camp even had the hostages in it? What were the odds Auger hadn't already been dumped off some place on a jungle trail, an expendable piece of baggage? Matt struggled to erase the negative thoughts from his mind. He had to make a decision. The shivering wasn't helping.

"All right, guys, let's get back into the water. We'll swim until we can determine the position of the camp then go back onshore. Boone I want you to be ready to use the M-911 from the edge of the river. I don't want to bump into any surprises so close to the camp. What kind of range can you get out of the scope?"

Oby answered for Boone, "You'll just be able to see camp fires and such sixty meters away."

Boone disagreed, "Fifty meters would be more like it boss, especially with no moon through these trees."

Matt understood, "Good then that is what we will do. We will keep moving down and checking with the scope. Boone you take point. Oby and I will move behind you. Don't worry about the other side of the river for right now, Oby. You take rear security and I'll focus on the right flank."

"You got it boss!" said Oby. The three SEALs eased back out into the river. The water seemed ten times colder now, Matt thought, sucking in his breath. They swam and bobbed in the shallows for eight minutes or so, bouncing off the muddy bottom. Matt couldn't ascertain from Boone's body language whether or not he was having success with the night vision scope. But then again Boone wasn't the type to demonstrate or act out his excitement if he did see something. He'd wait until he saw something absolutely positive and then he'd nonchalantly pass the word like it wasn't a big deal.

Matt heard Oby's teeth chattering behind him. All in all they'd been in the water for over five hours since starting the mission. He again looked at the luminescent face of his dive watch. The sun's rays would start painting the morning sky around five fifteen. An hour, he thought, only an hour to get set up. He realized he was flirting with the mission's expressed abort criteria. In the time they had left they were supposed to set up and observe the camp, report its location and status, and confirm the presence of the two American hostages. Matt wasn't sure they could pull it off.

Well, he was committed to trying, he thought. They owed it to Auger to make it work. While Matt was daydreaming Boone had stopped, Matt bumped into his point man.

Oby ran into Matt next. The three SEALs stood shivering, their weapons shaking but still held at the ready. Matt and Oby waited for Boone's verdict. Instead of saying anything, Boone raised his right hand touching two fingers to his eyes. The hand and arm signal communicated the fact that Boone was looking at the enemy.

Boone extended his index finger, pointing at the shoreline. He changed his hand position, spreading his fingers wide and slowly bringing them together until there was a very short distance between his fingertips and his thumb. That indicated the bad guys were very close, too close.

The shivering stopped immediately as the three SEALs adjusted their bodies to face the new threat. Matt and Oby moved up next to Boone. They both realized from the last hand signal that they must be so close that someone could hear or spot them any second. Boone quietly handed the night scope to Matt, carefully turning it off first so the green glow emanating from the eyepiece couldn't be seen. Matt placed the scope to his eye and turned on the M-911. He could instantly see three or four spots of light dancing through the trees. The spots of light he knew to be campfires from the way the light moved back and forth. He heard a sound that sounded like pots or pans being hit together. Then Matt saw the two men sitting on the edge of the river.

Matt couldn't take his attention away from the two guerillas. They appeared to be sleeping, slumped against the trunk of a large tree. He reached to his left and squeezed Boone's shoulder. Boone watched as Matt placed his free hand against his neck and made a cutting motion. Boone understood the command. He slid his hand across his chest and placed his hand on the rubberized grip of the pistol hanging under his left arm. Boone pulled the weapon out of its specially designed holster. The holster was extended to allow for the four-inch silencer.

Oby observed his friends body language and eased his weapon up. He wouldn't open fire unless Boone failed to take out the two men on the riverbank. Boone raised the pistol an inch at a time until he was finally sighting down the short black barrel. Normally, he'd double tap a target, placing two shots into each man. But he needed to finish these men in a total of just two rapidly aimed shots.

Boone squeezed the trigger, focusing on the front sight of the weapon. The pistol jumped in his hand as the first round was fired into the man on the left. Boone didn't wait to see the result of his marksmanship. He smoothly shifted his point of aim to the second man, taking up the trigger slack as he moved the weapon. The pistol spit out the second shot hitting the target squarely in the forehead. Both guerillas were dead and the SEALs were still behind schedule.

Matt swept the shoreline one more time before turning off the night vision scope. He didn't need to congratulate Boone. The point man knew this was only the beginning. Matt leaned toward Oby and cupped his hand around his ear. He brought the sniper up to speed on what had transpired. He then explained their next move. Matt then repeated the instructions to Boone. Boone was to move down the shoreline and closer to the camp. All three of the men knew they were in great jeopardy. Eventually, someone would come looking for the two dead men. Once the alarm was sounded the chance of rescue for General Alexander and Auger would be lost. The recon team's survival was also at risk, the three SEALs didn't have the firepower to fight a protracted battle if tracked down by searchers from the camp.

Matt had whispered to Boone and Oby that if detected the three of them should go under water and allow the river current to take them away from the camp. At the same time, they would try to swim diagonally across the river to make it to the opposite shore. They patrolled another fifteen minutes as Boone skillfully maneuvered the three SEALs up to where the jungle tree line touched the river. Boone used the M-911 to view the camp nestled in the horseshoe shaped clearing.

Matt and Oby, whose eyes were adjusted to the dark, could only pick out activity around the campfires. They observed several large dark objects, which Matt supposed were buildings. There were no sentries moving along the shoreline where at least three boats were tied up to a log reaching from the shore out into the river. Boone passed the scope to Matt for a better look at the camp. Matt turned the scope on. He could now clearly see one or two men moving around by one of the buildings. There were three or four people around one fire, and two or three others by the second fire.

The numbers added up to eleven or twelve guerillas. As Matt scanned the camp he spotted a small hill directly across the camp opening. On top of the hill he saw two dark square objects with a sentry standing next to them. Matt knew there was always a good reason to post a sentry, but his guess was there was something or someone up there on the hill the Columbians valued.

Matt scanned back down the hill and over to the other side where the encampment once again turned into jungle. The entrance facing the river was approximately seventy yards wide and the camp was cut about eighty yards deep. As soon as Matt completed his reconnaissance of the layout, he turned the night vision scope off and handed it to Oby. Oby repeated the drill until he also understood the layout of the camp. Matt checked the time—it was one minute after five.

Matt hadn't paid attention to the horizon but now as he glanced skyward he could see that the sky had changed from inky black to a soft gray. He now had to decide whether to stay on this side of the river or to move across to the original observation point. Matt realized that he wouldn't be able to get positive confirmation on the hostages until first light. Since they were already in a position where they could observe the details of the camp maybe it was best to stay where they were, next to the objective. Matt held on to Oby's shoulder and slowly pulled him toward the shore. He took the lead, crawling out of the river an inch at a time allowing the water to drain from his pants and his boots.

It took a full ten minutes for Matt to move his body on shore. Behind and next to him Boone and Oby were following suit. By five twenty, the three SEALs were huddled a few feet inside the jungle tree line waiting for the sun to rise. Matt felt around in his hip pouch until he located his binoculars. The night vision goggles would be useless now. The binoculars would give him enough detail to determine whether or not Senior Chief Auger and the general were in the camp.

Boone pulled out the emergency radio and shifted to the new daily changing frequency. He was prepared to send one burst coded signal indicating they had located the hostages. If they did not locate the hostages or realize that the hostages were not in the camp the three SEALs would pull away from the camp and go live on the net from a safe area and explain the situation to higher authority. For now all they could do was wait, wait until the sun came up, wait until they could confirm for sure their friend was still alive.

# CHAPTER ELEVEN

---

## In the sky over Columbia

The two MH-60 Black Hawk helicopters cruised side by side, quietly holding their final orbit. The SEAL platoon and its insertion package had been advanced methodically by the mission coordinators in the P-3 Orion high overhead. Lieutenant Stone and Chief Sampson had worked out a simple plan. They figured it was best to infiltrate by sliding down fast ropes half a mile away from the guerilla base camp. X-Ray's intelligence petty officer had detected a path on the satellite photos that ran along the river and straight into the encampment. It was a terrain feature the helicopter pilots could locate quickly from the air.

The hairpin loop in the path would be their insertion point and from there the platoon would patrol quickly down the path and into the camp. Stone was praying the reconnaissance team was in position to supply covering fire from the opposite side of the river. It would be very helpful to have some fellow frogmen out there knocking the bad guys down from the backside. Jared was a little worried about relying on people he'd never met to make the mission work. He had to take it on faith the SEALs in the small recon team would do their part.

Chief Sampson still had reservations about their ability to execute the plan of attack. Jared's own fears began to fade as the pre-mission adrenaline started to kick in and his ego took hold. The lieutenant knew what his SEAL platoon was capable of doing. The time for planning was over, it was time to earn their pay!

Lieutenant Stone checked his watch, it was five twenty-five in the morning. From the helicopter's viewpoint they could see the sun peeking over the far horizon. A voice crackled to life in his headset. "Lieutenant Stone we have a positive "go" command from headquarters. Code green, I say again, code green. The hostages have been located at the base camp location. You'd better get your SEALs back there ready to make it happen. We're going to be moving in fast, following the river at tree top level to mask the noise of our approach. Then we'll pop up violently over the landmark and drop you guys in. Are you ready?"

Lieutenant Stone's palms began to sweat. He really hadn't expected to hear the code word. Things usually didn't go this smoothly on SEAL missions. He had half expected the reconnaissance team to find the base camp full of young trainees practicing how to shoot. He acknowledged the insertion briefing. "Nothing wrong with a little violence of action flyboy! I'll let my guys know the deal, thanks!"

Jared took off the headset and turned to his nervous chief. "It's a go. Get the fast ropes ready." Sampson grinned.

"It's party time, LT! Lets lock and load!" The helicopter pilot relayed the code word to the second helicopter trailing them with the other half of X-Ray platoon. The Black Hawks were already dropping rapidly, moving from their orbit altitude to shoot in low across the Columbian countryside. In the distance the sun seemed to be rising way too quickly. The SEAL's hope had been they'd have the element of surprise by hitting the camp in the gray light of early morning. By Jared's best calculations he put them in the camp at approximately six forty-five. The guerrillas might still be groggy from sleeping in. They surely wouldn't expect someone hitting them from the jungle. The lieutenant checked his watch one more time before moving to the door.

## Jungle Rendezvous

The escort from the camp had been waiting at the rendezvous point for over an hour. Their leader was excited. He'd never met Chavez and it was certainly a great honor to personally meet him and escort him into their camp. The rumor going around was that Chavez was coming in to kill the hostages himself. Even so, both the hostages had been treated well. He'd placed a guard on them to ensure nothing would happen to them while he was away from the camp.

He'd already received a radio signal from the patrol escorting Chavez telling him they'd be at the rendezvous location in fifteen minutes. He tried to relax by getting his mind off the impending visit. He liked his life, it was simple but again everybody in Columbia led a simple life. His position in the guerilla army gave him dignity and a sense of purpose. He was a good leader, trusted and respected by his men. If he handled himself well today he might even get a chance to work for Chavez. They all knew Chavez looked for talent and if chosen, a man could advance as a member of the inner circle.

At the very least he should receive a promotion. A promotion meant being put in charge of more men, possibly a sector of his very own to control. It wasn't about money or rank. It was about power. He was ready and maybe, just maybe, Chavez would think so too.

The two MH-60s flew in low, skimming twenty feet over the water, one helicopter at point and the second close behind. The Black Hawk leader was using his navigation system to determine the exact location of the insertion point. The light from the blossoming dawn helped the army pilot to identify key terrain features in the jungle and the surrounding hills. According to the map, the large bend in the river trail should be very easy to see.

The insertion plan was going to lean heavily on established procedures. Nothing fancy. Pop up to an altitude of a hundred feet, three hundred yards short of the loop in the trail. The Black Hawk shifted upward in small increments until it reached an altitude of one hundred feet. In clipped professional tones the lead helicopter pilot explained where he was and what he was about to do. Since they'd already gone through the entire mission in the simulator the other pilot understood exactly what was going down but they still had to communicate on final approach.

The lead Black Hawk slowed down, the pilot had spotted the sharp turn in the trail. His aim point for the fast rope was where the path came closest to the river. He dipped the nose and plunged toward the mark. Seconds later the Black Hawk pulled its nose up and hovered in midair.

## Guerilla Base Camp–Ariari River

Matt couldn't take the binoculars away from his eyes. As soon as enough sunlight illuminated the camp, he was able to detect movement inside the dark squares and see they were cages. One cage held an older heavyset man in a tattered green uniform. He was moving around and trying to communicate to the man in the other cage.

The other man, even from this distance, was easily recognizable. It was Senior Chief Auger and he was alive. Matt quickly grabbed Boone and handed him the binoculars. Boone looked for a second and then handed the binoculars back. He'd already picked up the radio beacon, checked the frequency setting, and sent out the signal telling the higher command authority the hostages were indeed in the camp.

Although the three men hadn't discussed it out loud each was going over in his mind what he thought the rescue team would do. Where it would infiltrate, whether or not it would assault directly into the middle of the camp or land somewhere outside and patrol into the fight. Matt, Oby and Boone were not privy to the rescue plan, an intelligent precaution in case they were captured during the recon mission.

Matt was focused on keeping the two Americans alive until help arrived. From this point on they were on standby to assist. Oby could effectively use his modified rifle to provide sniper cover from their position in the trees. The first thing Matt would have him do was drop the sentry on the hill. Adding a few insurance rounds in him for good measure to make damned sure he couldn't harm the two hostages. From that point, anybody going near that hill was a dead man.

## Insertion point

Lieutenant Jared Stone grabbed the top of the furry rope and kicked the carefully coiled pile out of the Black Hawk. There is no time to think during a fast rope assault. He rotated his body around the rope and started to slide. He wore two sets of gloves; a wool pair to disperse heat, and a leather pair the protect his hands. The fast rope was a British invention that allowed people to slide down much like firemen sliding down a fire pole. If done right, the eight men of his SEAL squad would be on the ground in three to four seconds.

They'd trained to this task over and over again as part of their hostage rescue training and are able to execute the dynamic operation in a very small area such as a rooftop or a jungle trail. Upon hitting the ground they deployed into a defensive perimeter, providing cover for the last men coming down the rope. Both Black Hawks placed the men down simultaneously, the powerful aircraft only thirty feet apart. Within seconds the SEAL squads were on the ground and the air crews cut the fast ropes free to fall to the trail below. The ropes were expendable and the helicopters didn't want to risk getting them entangled in a tall jungle tree as they departed the insertion area.

The Black Hawks banked away heading off to a new orbit position nearby. They were configured as gun ships, and were destined to return later to recover the hostages and provide covering fire for the SEAL platoon. Stone hoped the reconnaissance team was in position to help him attack the camp. He knew the recon team had their own extraction plan but he thought his fellow SEALs would want to hitch a ride on the helicopters. There was enough room in the helicopters to squeeze in the three recon men, but just barely.

From the center of his own squad's perimeter, Chief Sampson gave Jared a thumbs up, communicating a full head count and readiness to get underway. The chief was the assistant patrol leader and as such he commanded his own eight-man squad. The SEAL leaders had planned this part of the operation down to its smallest detail, so far, so good.

Their intention was to depart immediately, forming a double file with one squad on either side of the path. They offset the squads so each SEAL could engage the enemy to the left and right, without striking their buddy. A heavy two man lead element consisting of a point man and an M-60 gunner gave the formation added punch. Anyone bumping into the Americans on the trail would get more than a black eye. X-Ray platoon needed to "unass" the landing zone ASAP. It was possible the helicopter insertion could've bee heard by the guerillas in the base camp seven hundred yards away. Lieutenant Stone signaled Chief Sampson to stand up and create the formation. The two squads moved together as one, the point element advancing a good four yards ahead of the main body.

## *The Rendezvous Point*

The young guerrilla leader sat watching in awe as the Americans appeared directly over his ten man camp escort. He was even more surprised when he saw bodies sliding down ropes into the jungle only yards away from he and his ten man group. They knew he had to deal with this intrusion. The Americans obviously knew about the linkup with Chavez and it was up to him to protect Chavez. The VIP was due to arrive any minute so he had to strike now! If he could eliminate these soldiers he would be a hero to both his men and to Chavez.

The other nine men were staring up at the helicopters in amazement, not one had his weapon at the ready. The young leader turned and whispered his battle instructions to the Columbians directing them to quickly deploy around the curve of the trail. Just in case the American's real target was the camp, he set up an L-shaped ambush to cover two directions of movement. All he had to do now was to wait.

Not far away, Chavez and his patrol stopped abruptly as the helicopters passed overhead. The drug lord glanced up and instantly recognized the aircraft for what they were, American Special Operations helicopters, MH-60 Black Hawks. Were they after him, he wondered with alarm, or were they after the hostages? He suddenly realized that his revenge could be short circuited by the arrival of the Americans. He was too close to let this happen.

Chavez owed it to his dead son to finish the job, to have final vengeance. He moved quickly up the narrow trail and grabbed the patrol leader by the shirt. Chavez ordered him to move as fast as possible to the rendezvous point. The patrol leader nodded fearfully and gave the command for his men to follow quickly. Chavez and the twenty-five guerrillas jogged down the trail with their weapons at the ready. They were only a minute or two away from the rendezvous point.

## River Base Camp

Only minutes before, Oby had received a coded radio message sent by a P-3 Orion fixed wing command and control aircraft circling over the area of operation. The message confirmed a SEAL platoon was on the ground heading to the base camp. Matt's orders were to assist in the rescue, if possible, and to link up with the SEAL platoon for extraction after the hostages were recovered. Matt would be able to communicate only by relaying through the P-3. Nobody in the camp appeared to be aware of the American force closing in.

An explosive blast of automatic gunfire erupted in the distance. Matt recognized the distinct signature of an ambush. The SEAL platoon hadn't initiated the contact he realized, they would've employed claymore mines as vital part of their attack. Could the SEAL platoon be under attack? The sounds of gunfire increased in volume and intensity, growing into a full pitched battle in the Columbian jungle.

The remaining guerrillas in the camp were running out of their huts. The sentry on the hill was suddenly alert and nervously looking around, wondering what instructions he'd be given about the hostages. Oby pulled the stock of his sniper rifle tightly into his shoulder and drew a bead on the confused sentry. "Hold off a little, Oby," Matt said. "Let's wait and see what happens here."

"No sweat, boss," Oby replied, speaking out of the corner of his mouth. He relaxed his trigger finger but kept the cross hairs on the sentry's chest. Matt felt helpless as he listened to the gun battle raging hundreds of yards away. Whatever was going on it couldn't be good, he realized. A rescue force wasn't supposed to get into a pitched battle this far from its objective.

Boone reached over and pulled Matt close to him. "You know, boss, they may not even make it here. What do you say we take a shot at grabbing the senior chief?" Matt stared at Boone in disbelief. He hadn't even considered the possibility of the SEAL platoon failing, but Boone was right. It sounded crazy, but then again, they were in a position to try. If the other SEALs failed to reach the camp the Columbians would jettison the hostages and disband, spreading out into the jungle to fight again another day.

The recon team wasn't carrying a lot of firepower. Each SEAL had ninety rounds for his primary assault rifle. Oby had fifty extra rounds for his sniper rifle and Boone had thirty down loaded bullets for his silenced pistol. If Oby stayed on the long gun, Boone and Matt would have to provide the volume of fire needed to gain fire superiority. It would be critical for the three SEALs to employ greater violence of action than the Columbians. Only in that way could they intimidate the guerillas into running or hiding, giving Matt time to attempt a rescue.

The SEAL lieutenant thought the adhoc plan through phase by phase. There were only fifteen or so guerrillas in the camp. With a little luck his small team should be able to drop at least five or six of the Columbians right off the bat. But there was no way around the fact the three SEALs would have to move across open ground under direct fire from the enemy to reach the hostages on the hill. Once on the hill they would be exposed for at least three minutes trying to recover the two Americans from the cages. If even one of them were wounded they'd be in deep shit. They wouldn't have enough men to fight and carry the wounded man simultaneously.

"Forget about it," Matt said. "The SEAL platoon will be here as planned. Let's stick to helping them achieve their mission."

"Whatever you say, sir, you're the boss!" Oby answered back sarcastically. Matt didn't take it personally. He knew there was an outside chance he and his small team might have still have to attempt the impossible. He offered Oby some guidance.

"Oby, if that sentry swings his weapon toward the cages I want you to drop him! If anyone else approaches the base of that hill it's nap time, got it?"

"Roger that, boss. I'm looking inside his ear right now." Matt smiled, leave it to Oby to be a step ahead.

## Jungle Trail-Columbia

When the hot blast of ripping lead screeched across the trail, the tail end of the SEAL platoon's formation had immediately gone to ground returning fire. Chief Sampson's squad was just outside the kill zone and immediately swung to the left like a gate opening. They brought withering fire down on the ambusher's flank. The point man in front of Jared had been wounded in the first volley. The M-60 gunner had also been hit but he was still returning fire, operating the large belt fed weapon like a pro.

Luckily for the SEALs the guerrillas hadn't picked a very good ambush site. The Columbians were located behind a five-foot high ridge paralleling the trail. It was a great defensive position elevated slightly above the path. However, once the Americans went to ground most of the bullets were flying two feet above. The Columbians had to stand up to aim down at the road where the platoon lay.

A few of the SEALs figured this out right away and began lobbing fragmentation grenades over the ridgeline. Several others picked off the Columbians whenever they stood up to fire. The Americans were also at a disadvantage. From the trail they were unable to apply direct firepower on the ambushers, not without standing up themselves. Two SEALs crawled to the wounded point element creating a four-man fire team. The M-60 gunner could move under his own power so he and another

SEAL continued fighting. The fourth man dragged the badly wounded point man down the trail and out of the kill zone, staying low to avoid being hit.

Lieutenant Stone popped a red star cluster round into the M-203 grenade launcher mounted underneath his carbine and shot the round into the sky. He didn't have the radio and there wasn't time to find his radioman. The signal would communicate to the orbiting helicopters that the SEALs on the ground required emergency fire support. The SEALs in the kill zone kept inching themselves out of the ambush site. A few curious guerrillas poked their heads up to see what was happening. It was a big mistake.

On the flank Chief Sampson took full advantage. Three or four of the SEALs were picking off the guerrillas as they exposed themselves. The SEAL platoon began to break contact, each man pushing himself on his belly towards the river. Several SEALs were now wounded. Stone's squad rejoined the rest of the platoon as they continued their movement back. With three men wounded and six men dragging them Jared had only seven men fighting. He had no way of knowing how many guerillas were dead and had to think worse case. In all probability the SEALs were out numbered.

The roaring sound of the Black Hawks coming in close and low, cut through the sound of the gunfire. The guerrilla leader realized their prey had escaped the ambush and were still capable of fighting. Now he had to deal with the Americans in the air. The odds had turned against him in the blink of an eye. The lead MH-60 door gunner could clearly see the guerrillas arrayed along the ridge. He could also see the SEALs moving slowly toward the river. He passed on to the pilot that it looked like some of the SEALs were wounded.

As the pilot relayed that information back to the command control element the door gunner opened on the Columbians, watching the angry tracers rip into three of the guerillas. The second Black Hawk circled around to the opposite side of the guerrilla position and began pounding them unmercifully. A constant stream of machinegun bullets was shredding the jungle all around the enemy. The ground at their feet came alive as it jumped and popped with the impact of the rounds.

The lead Black Hawk circled back around strafing the jungle. The second bird rotated out to the river to get a view of the SEAL platoon's progress. A plinking sound alerted the pilot of the lead helicopter that he was taking ground fire. The door gunner yelled into his headset microphone that he had more bad guys swarming up the trail, twenty to twenty-five moving fast. He reiterated this was a new enemy force. The Black Hawks were taking heavy fire now. The Columbians might be having problems finding the SEALs, but the helicopters were easy targets. The lead pilot realized the birds couldn't stay in close contact with the ground battle without risking loss of a gunship. They needed to stay battle effective to extract the SEALs and possibly rescue the two hostages. The pilot passed the situation back to higher command via the P-3.

## Base Camp–Ariari River

Oby, Matt, and Boone watched the red star cluster arc up into the sky and slowly fall to the ground. They listened helplessly as the Black Hawks supported the beleaguered SEAL platoon. Matt realized there was no chance the rescue force could get to the camp before some enterprising Columbian ordered the hostages killed. There was nothing left to consider, Matt made his decision. "Oby, take that sentry out now!" Before the last word was spoken Oby's rifle jumped in his hands. The sentry slumped to the ground, struck in the head. The SEALs got away with this first move without being detected. Most of the guerrillas in the camp were standing around nervously staring toward the battle not far away. Oby shifted gears and took out the guerrilla closest to the base of the hill. So far, so good.

Matt and Boone both moved up on line and opened fire, each taking a man. They aimed and squeezed and aimed again, making sure they didn't miss. It was only a matter of time before the guerrillas found the three frogmen. The SEALs continued firing until seven of the guerrillas lay motionless on the ground. Then one of the guerrillas realized they were taking fire from behind. The remaining guerrillas scrambled to get their weapons. Here we go, Matt thought. They had to make their move to save the hostages before the Columbians maneuvered against them. Matt jumped up and yelled, "Let's move!"

Boone and Oby grabbed their gear and jumped to their feet. They sprinted alongside their officer, spraying bullets toward the center of camp to dissuade the guerrillas from taking aim. The SEALs passed the boats tied up along the shoreline and raced up the side of the small hill toward the cages. Auger had watched the progress of the confused guerrillas moving around the camp. It looked like the Columbians were trying to decide if they should stay and defend the camp or go to the aid of the escort patrol. He was startled as the sentry guarding them flipped backwards, dropping to the ground in front of his cage. A small red hole in the man's head oozed blood. A chill ran down his spine. Somebody was out there. Somebody close.

"General, General Alexander!" he called out.

The general shifted around until he had eye contact with Auger, "Yes, senior chief?"

"General we have help coming, get ready. Anything could happen now." Just then Auger saw three or four more bodies drop to the ground in the base camp. He wasn't sure if the gun battle in the jungle was a diversion but he knew that somebody was already here and they were taking care of business. Auger saw more movement down to his right near the river. Looking down the hill he watched three men dash from the jungle tree line, three men he recognized instantly. Boone was the first man on top of the hill.

"What's this? The chief's mess?" Boone was grinning from ear to ear despite the strain he was under. How you doing, senior chief?"

"A lot happier now that I see your ugly ass!' Auger responded. Oby and Matt cleared the top of the hill and spun around. They immediately opened fire on the Columbians running toward them. Oby broke off his conversation with Auger and went to ground. He aimed and punched a round through the man giving orders down below. He adjusted his aim to the left taking out a guerilla firing from behind a shed.

Oby muttered to himself, those idiots don't realize the thin wood wouldn't stop a bullet passing through and killing a man. Boone and Matt crawled to the cages pulling their knives from their sheaths. The two men efficiently cut the cords holding the cage doors shut. They reached in and pulled out Senior Chief and General Alexander. Neither man could stand up at first. Matt glanced around quickly from his hill top position. They could move down the hill but then they would have to carry the senior chief and the general wherever they went. Back in the center of camp, three of the guerrillas were getting smarter, maneuvering from cover to cover to get closer to the SEALs.

Then it hit him. The answer was right in front of him. The boats! "Boone! Send the "hostages rescued" code word to the P-3!" Matt hoped the SEAL platoon would be able to disengage and extract once they knew the hostages were in friendly hands.

Boone finished the call. "Boss, they want to know where we want to be picked up?" Matt thought for a moment.

"Down river, Boone! Tell them we'll request pickup down river!" Matt's plan was simple. Get everybody to the boats and put distance between the Columbians and the SEAL recon team as fast as possible. Matt directed Oby and Boone to help the general and the senior chief get down the hill. Then Matt sprinted towards the line of boats, firing in the direction of a pair of approaching guerrillas.

Matt reached the boats and dove panting to the ground. He tried to regain his composure and take aim on yet another pesky Columbian sneaking up the right tree line. The guerrilla poked his head out and was surprised to see Matt, lying next to the boats. He was even more surprised when he was blown backward by the round going into his chest. Matt changed magazines and untied the boats.

# CHAPTER TWELVE

Chavez and his small escort slashed their way through the dense jungle and he found himself tiring rapidly. The shooting up ahead escalated in volume and intensity. The violent sounds of the life and death struggle echoed through the jungle. Chavez broke through the last veil of foliage and arrived abruptly in the middle of a battle.

Most of his expected guerrilla escort from the base camp lay tossed like rags on the trail. A few were moving here and there, but most were dead. Chavez was furious. His first thought was that somehow the Columbian military had double-crossed him. Attempting to ambush him far away from his high paid bodyguards and network of informants. He didn't suspect the Americans.

Bullets ripped the ground at Chavez's feet showering him with debris. He drove to the right and rolled, screaming a command.

"Open fire!"

His escort was already going to ground and didn't need their leader's prompting. They returned a withering barrage of firepower, sweeping their weapons to increase the impact area. Two young Columbians jumped up and ran directly toward the Americans. Making them perfect targets for the waiting SEALs. The SEAL s however, weren't the only threat.

The first Black Hawk helicopter finished extracting the second squad of X-Ray platoon and completed a tight turn, diving in low and fast. The strafing took the escort and Chavez by surprise, focused as they were on the SEALs straight ahead. The two men attacking the SEALs were thrown back violently as the miniguns tore into them. Chavez threw himself back just in time to avoid being cut in half by the angry 7.62 rounds stitching across the trail. The guerilla next to him wasn't as lucky. Chavez was sprayed with the man's hot blood. A boy in front of Chavez screamed.

The American commandos on the ground were moving fast. Two SEALs jumped up ran across the trail, firing on the run. The SEALs still on the ground covered the flanking move by increasing their volume of fire. The Columbians hugged the dirt to avoid the withering fire but more were hit by the SEALs deadly assault. Chavez heard a weird screeching sound. He looked up to spot yet another American helicopter diving toward their position.

Things were going badly here. The Americans aggressively moved forward four or five yards at a time. Their tactic was simple. Assault pairs jumped forward and went to ground. As they opened up the next pair moved forward. There was never a lull in the roaring punishment meted out by their automatic weapons. The Columbians were just lying there, unable to lift their heads for fear of being shot.

At this rate, between the ground troops and the helicopters, Chavez and his late arrivals would be wiped out in no time. Something had to be done! He grabbed the three closest men and yelled at a fourth man squatting nearby.

"Follow me! We must head for the base camp! Move, move, MOVE!" Despite his fatigue and the fear clawing at his belly, Chavez dug down deep and rallied his men.

The Columbians were only too happy to obey. None of them wished to remain here to die. The five Columbians smashed into the jungle running behind Chavez at full speed. The branches ripped and tore at their clothes as they struggled to put distance between them and the American death trap on the trail. The SEALs shifted their fire, tracking the escaping men as they left the kill zone.

Chavez stayed low as the bullets buzzed all around him like angry bees. As the small patrol ripped through the jungle he began formulating a new plan of action. They would loop around and head for the base camp. There were more forces there, enough to protect Chavez. Besides, he had a task to complete in the camp. Fear of dying hadn't clouded his reason for being here in harms way.

Then another chilling thought struck him. What if the Americans held the camp? He had no way of knowing. No way to call and find out if the camp was safe! Chavez decided to strike for the river instead. Once there he'd work his way back to the camp and check out the situation first hand.

## The River Base Camp

General Alexander and Auger lay motionless in the bottom of the crude boat. The general groaned, "Jesus, I can't move my legs!"

"Don't worry general," Auger observed. "Your muscles need more time to work the kinks out. There's nothing for you to do and nowhere to go, so I recommend you just relax and enjoy the ride! And by the way general, I prefer Coors! Make it a case of long neck bottles!" Beside the boat, Boone and Oby were firing and changing magazines as if on autopilot. The two navy men pounded the camp, laying down a deadly accurate rain of lead. Their marksmanship had already evened the odds. The few remaining guerillas were hiding, grouped near an old rusty generator. They were trying to work up enough gumption to counter attack. The problem was every time one of them stuck out his head, he was nailed by the two riflemen laying on the riverbank.

The leader of the little group screamed at the men to have courage and fight back. In frustration, he threw up his hands and ordered the others to stay behind the generator. He knew this game of cat and mouse could only last as long as the SEAL's ammunition held out.

Matt tugged and pulled at the boat until finally it began to drift into shallow water. Back on shore Oby and Boone continued snapping off aimed shots. They were running out of ammunition. Matt decided it was time to leave.

"Oby! Boone, fall back! Let's move it!" By now Matt was in chest deep water, trying to keep the now mobile boat from spinning away in the fast current.

"Come on!" urged Auger. Boone was first to react to the command. "Boone going back! Boone is going back!" Boone scooted backwards until his feet were wet then turned around. Boone moved into chest deep water and opened fire.

"Go Oby! Go, go, go!" Oby dropped another guerilla with a well-placed shot to the chest and rolled to the right entering the river and clearing Boone's field of fire.

"Here I come!" Oby wiggled his way past Boone while his partner kept the bad guys honest. Matt was on the tip of his toes he knew he was losing control of the boat.

He needed help. "Auger! Grab the radio and call the Black Hawks for covering fire! Have them hit the camp!" Matt watched as Boone reached the boat and hauled himself into the boat. Boone twisted around and lobbed a forty-millimeter grenade into the camp. Oby's hand clamped onto the edge of the boat. General Alexander took Oby's rifle and helped the sniper flip into the shallow craft.

Auger flipped the cover off the pack back containing the UHF radio and tried to raise the gun ships. "Red Dog Three, Red Dog Three, we need fire placed on the base camp, over. I say again fire mission, over!"

Matt pulled himself out of the river and into the boat even as the craft spun three hundred and sixty degrees. He landed with a thump right on top of the general, whacking him in the head with his rifle. "Sorry sir!" General Alexander rubbed his bruised forehead.

"There's not a lot of room in this tub lieutenant but it's damn sure better than walking! Are you the last man we need to pick up?"

"Yes, sir, the navy felt sending three SEALs was more than sufficient to do the job!" The general laughed.

"Yes, it seems I've grossly underestimated you SEAL types!"

Matt wasn't sure what the general meant but he was too busy to find out just now. He turned his attention back to Auger's efforts to raise the helicopters.

The boat was really starting to move much faster so near the center of the river. Back in the camp the Columbians hiding behind the generator realized the Americans had stopped firing. They ran toward the river frantically yelling for others to come out of hiding and join them. Their leader watched as the boat drifted past the camp and out of sight.

"Red Dog Three, do you read me, over?" Auger checked the frequency setting again. He scanned the laminated fire support card attached to the radio. Everything was as it should be. Then fate answered his call for help.

"Red Dog Three is on egress frogman. They're bingo fuel and ammo. We are SPECTRE One Five, in orbit over your position. Confirm your request to hit the camp, over."

"Hey boss we've got an air force fixed wing gunship topside!" Auger had reason to be excited. The SPECTRE gun ships were armed with heavy firepower. They controlled their fire by using a computer aided aiming system. Matt looked at the sky. He knew the gunship operated from a relatively low orbit.

"Tell him to hit the camp. All the good guys are clear." Matt was interrupted by the sound of bullets popping overhead. The Columbians had reached the shoreline. They were terrible shots. "Auger!"

"Roger that, boss! SPECTRE One Five, hit the camp now, we are taking heavy fire from the shoreline. Do you copy, over?"

"Roger your last, frogman, we confirm target. Standby." The voice was monotone and business like. The SEALs kept low. They all heard what sounded like paper ripping. Matt watched the shoreline fading in the distance as the ground around the Columbians suddenly erupted in flame and flying dirt. The SPECTRE's guns operated so fast Matt couldn't hear separate rounds being fired. The ripping sound was the gun ship's unique song of death.

Chavez and his small bodyguard stopped dead in their tracks. The SPECTRE seemed to be right on top of them. Chavez needed to see what was going on. "We must hurry! There will be reinforcements in the camp. Hurry!" The men acknowledged his order but they were near exhaustion. They continued to thrash through the jungle until he heard the sound of rushing water.

"Companions! The river, I hear it just ahead! Faster now, faster!" The guerillas accompanying Chavez took heart from the news. Soon they would be safely in the camp with their comrades. Chavez began to see flashes of water through the trees. He signaled for the others to advance ahead of him and slowed to a walk. By his estimation they should come out of the jungle one hundred meters or so down stream from the camp. Chavez mulled over the calls he'd have to make. He needed time to regroup and rethink his strategy. The general could wait a bit longer.

Boone took time to check over both the senior chief, and the general, to make sure they were unharmed by their long ordeal. He gently probed down the length of their bodies looking for broken bones or wounds. Everything checked out okay. Although both men looked terrible, they were very much alive and would recover with a little sleep and some hot food.

Suddenly, Oby sounded the alarm. Boone whipped around, bringing up his rifle. "Hey, boys, looks like we've got company!" Oby pointed toward the shoreline just ahead of their position. Matt signaled for Auger and General Alexander to stay low. He could see a group of guerillas standing on the shoreline.

"What's the call, boss?" Oby was ready. His sniper rifle steadied on the side of the boat.

Matt looked at the new arrivals through his binoculars. Three of the men were guerillas. The fourth man looked different, suddenly he recognized the man. It was Chavez! Matt had a thought.

"Oby, Boone, drop the three to the left. Leave the fourth one on the right alive."

"You got it, sir!" Boone's words were drowned out by the explosive sound of both SEALs opening up on their assigned targets. The first two Columbians were hit in the chest. Both spun wildly and fell forward into the river. The third Columbian stood perfectly still, his face registering shock. The guerilla was confused, thinking the SEALs in the familiar boat were friends from the base camp. Boone snapped off another shot. The third man pitched backwards violently.

Matt focused on Chavez—now lying on the ground trying to play dead. "Senior chief! Give me the hand set!" Auger handed Matt the radio hand set as ordered.

"SPECTRE One Five, we have one more target. Do you copy, over?" Matt hoped the sophisticated weapons platform was still in town.

"That's a roger, frog boys, what can we do for you?" Matt gave SPECTRE the coordinates. The boat was moving around a bend in the river and Matt didn't have much time left to spot for the gunship. Operation Green Dagger was coming to a close.

Chavez was frozen in fear. One of the men serving as his escort lay nearby, a gaping hole in his head. He was a dead man if he stayed where he was but he was petrified. Chavez had to do something. Making his decision Chavez jumped to his feet and turned toward the jungle tree line behind him. Suddenly a loud ripping sound exploded overhead, freezing him in place. The Columbian glanced skyward in horror.

The SEALs watched in awe as the tree line erupted. A withering firestorm consisting of thousands of twenty-millimeter bullets pounded an area on the shore the size of a basketball court. The designated kill zone was saturated, the SPECTRE's vicious electric guns delivering one bullet for every square inch of ground. The concentrated gunship fire worked along the riverbank, blasting a smoking trench where Chavez had stood only seconds earlier. As suddenly as it started, the blizzard of lead stopped. A shapeless pile of rags lay in the center of the target box. Chavez would never deliver his personal justice.

Boone was the first to speak, "Geez, boss, nothing like a little overkill! I mean it was only one guy! I could've popped him easy." Matt considered his next words carefully.

"Overkill? I don't think so, Boone. That was Chavez. Overkill was too good for that son of a bitch!" Matt handed the hand set back to Senior Chief Auger.

"Boys, let's go home!"

Exhaustion washed over Matt as the boat made its way southward. He realized he loved this shit. The fear, the challenges, the whole damn thing. He'd been thinking a lot about his future and had come to a decision. Tina and their plans of a life together would have to be put on hold. Matt was a warrior, a navy SEAL. It was his destiny.

# EPILOGUE

The octagon shaped room was located deep inside the central intelligence agency headquarters building at Langley, Virginia. The lights were kept artificially low on purpose to make it difficult for newcomers to see who might be sitting inside. The effect also made it easy for those in the room to get a good look at a confused newcomer as he or she entered the darkened interior.

Two men sat in the room. The door was closed so they wouldn't be disturbed. A well-dressed gentleman in his mid-forties thumbed through a thick dossier, studying its contents. The other man was much older. Gray well established at the temples. He was clearly a man grown soft by too many years behind a desk.

The older man spoke first. "Well, sir, what do you think of our proposed candidate?" He was uncomfortable. He hated bringing in these political appointees to decide if the CIA was on the right track.

The other man looked up. "He's a good choice, Sam. I really think you nailed this one." Sam sat a little taller upon hearing the unexpected praise.

"I know he doesn't meet the minimum ten year service requirement, but sir, I've had him checked out every way I know how. He's rock solid as far as we're concerned."

The younger man closed the file folder. "Sam, in four or five years this SEAL officer's seen more action and had more relevant experience than some of the people we have in the program right now. I think you should bring him in, start the indoctrination process. Of course it's still his choice. Last I time I checked this was still a volunteer unit."

Sam nodded. "Yes sir. Of course he'd have to volunteer. But nobody's ever turned us down."

"Well you are right there, Sam. Why did you bring this second file?"

Sam looked down at the other folder. "Oberman? Well the lieutenant's a SEAL. SEALs don't work alone, never have. I thought Barrett might feel more comfortable joining us if had a friendly face in the unit. Oberman's a sniper and we just happen to have a sniper position open in the unit right now. Why not sweeten the deal for Barrett? Make them a buddy team!"

The younger man pondered the second file. "Sam, maybe you're right. These two men can be very useful to us." He shut the folder and looked at Sam. "All right, I'll give you the green light on these two. Start the wheels in motion. What's their status right now?"

Sam breathed a sigh of relief. "Sir, they're being debriefed on the Columbian operation as we speak. I'll get in touch with them right away."

"Good! Fine! Sam, I'm going to monitor these two candidates personally. I'm afraid the way things are going we'll have a lot of work for your Black Talon team. Maybe too much work."

0-595-27347-5

Printed in the United States
1332700002B/544